HERMAN

Hot Shared Wife Erotica

Just Plain Bob

WARNING

This book contains sexually explicit scenes and adult language. It may be considered offensive to some readers. This book is for sale to adults ONLY.

Please store your files wisely where they cannot be accessed by underage readers.

About the Publisher

4Fun Publishing, a member of **BLVNP Incorporated**, 340 S. Lemon #6200, Walnut CA 91789, info@blvnp.com / legal@blvnp.com

NOTE: Due to the highly emotional reaction of some people to works of erotic fiction, any email sent to the above address that contains foul language or religious references is automatically deleted by our anti-spam software and will not be seen. All other communications are welcome.

DISCLAIMER

Please don't be stupid and kill yourself. This book is a work of FICTION. Do not try any new sexual practice that you find in this book. It is fiction and not to be confused with reality. Neither the author nor the publisher or its associates assume any responsibility for any loss, injury, death or legal consequences resulting from acting on the contents in this book. Every character in this book is over 18 years of age. The author's opinions are not to be construed as the opinions of the publisher. The material in this book is for entertainment purposes ONLY. Enjoy.

Herman

Hot Shared Wife Erotica

By: Just Plain Bob

© Just Plain Bob 2015
ISBN: 978-1-68030-508-1

Chapter 1

I was sitting at a table in the student cafeteria eating lunch and reviewing the notes I'd taken during Mallory's Business Law III when someone pulled out a chair and sat down across from me. I looked up and into the most startling blue eyes I had ever seen. They belonged to a girl I'd never seen before. Actually she wasn't a girl, she was a woman. I'd guess maybe twenty-four or twenty-five.

"Harold, right?" She asked.

"No," I replied, "It's Herman."

"Sorry. I'll have to thump the person I got my information from. I wonder what else I got wrong from my source. May I call you Herm?"

I nodded my head yes and she said, "You are a Business Management major, you live in the dorms, are here on a half a dozen scholarships, work in the school cafeteria for spending money. Again, right?"

"Not completely. I don't live in the dorms. I have a house. The rest of it is right."

"No car and don't have enough money to date much. That about right?"

I nodded another yes and then asked, "Who are you and what is this all about?"

"My name is Samantha and I want to offer you a job."

"What kind of a job?"

"An actor in a porn flick."

"What?!!!"

"You heard me right. An actor in several porn films with me. They are specialty films and as such they require a certain feel to them and you are perfect for what I need. I'll need you maybe two nights a week for about six weeks and I'll give you five hundred a week. Think about it. I have a one o'clock in the Harris Building so I have to run, but if you are interested meet me at O'Malley's at seven tonight. Hope to see you there," and she stood up and left.

As she walked away I scoped out her marvelous ass as I rolled the "I want you to act in several porn films with me" in my mind. I hadn't been laid in a year and the thought of me being buried in that ass, even if it was being filmed, did appeal to me.

She disappeared through the cafeteria doors and as I turned back to my lunch and my notes, I wondered who the asshole was who was playing jokes on me. I put it out of my mind and concentrated on my notes on contract law.

***

Even knowing that I was going to be the butt of a practical joke, I still showed up at O'Malley's to see what the next part of the joke would be. I walked into the place expecting to see half a dozen of my friends waiting for me with big smiles and waiting to say "Gotcha" and laugh. I didn't see a soul that I knew except for the girl who said her name was Samantha.

She was alone in a booth toward the back and there were no people in the booths around her. As I took the seat across from her, she smiled at me and said:

"You came. Does that mean you are interested?"

"To be honest I'm here because I was thinking that I was being set up for a practical joke and I was curious to see what the next part of it would be."

"No joke, Herm. I was dead serious about what I said to you in the cafeteria. I need someone just like you to work with me in a series of porn films."

"Someone just like me?"

"No lies here, Herm, and I don't want you to take this wrong, but you have the look that I'm looking for. You are attractive enough to have drawn the attention of a girl like me, but you also look a little on the wimpish side and that's what I need. A guy that it would be reasonable to believe that he could have a girl like me, but who also looks like he could be bossed around. Pussy whipped I believe is the term used."

"Pussy whipped?"

"Have you heard the term 'cuckolded husband'?"

I nodded a yes.

"There is a big demand for cuckold type photo galleries and films. I can give you the addresses of a dozen sites that follow that genre. I want to make a series of those types of films and galleries and I need someone to play the part of the cuckolded husband."

"You want to pay me five hundred a week to pretend to be your husband and fuck you?"

"No, Herm, I don't want to mislead you on this, but I'll be paying you to act as my husband, but you won't be fucking me."

"I don't understand."

"You do know what a cuckold is, right?"

She saw from my facial expression that I wasn't sure so she went on, "One definition of a cuckold is a man who knowingly lets his woman fuck other men. A good cuck will watch and even help out."

"Help out?"

"Guide the other men's cocks into his wife. Clean her out after it is over."

"Clean her out?"

"You know; go down on her and suck all the goo out of her."

"Sorry. Don't think I can do that."

"You don't have to. That's why it is called acting. You get down into place and then the camera is positioned so that it looks like you are doing it."

"I don't know. It doesn't sound like something I could do."

"Sure you can. You will do maybe four hours' worth of work and get five hundred. That's one twenty-five an hour and you can't beat that with a stick."

"I still don't understand what I'd have to do."

"Basically you stand around looking like a wimp while I treat you like my personal servant. I'll give you an overview of one of the first films in the series. You are having a poker game at the house. I was supposed to go out for the night, but things fell through and I decided to stay home and act as hostess. A couple of hours into the game and after every one has had several drinks, one of the guys will say something like "You look good enough to eat, Bonnie." Bonnie is my screen name and I'll say something like "You any good at it?" The guy will say that he has never had any complaints and then I'll say that I'm just going to have to see for myself."

"Everyone at the table will look at look at you and then I'll say, "Bobby won't mind, will you, honey?" Bobby is going to be your screen name by the way. You will look like you want to puke, but you will say something along the lines of "Of course not, dear. Whatever you want" and the guy and I will leave the room. The other guys at the table will say things like, "She do this often?" or maybe "You let her get away with shit like this?" You will mumble something like "I can't stop her." They will look at you disgusted and then the camera cuts to the bedroom where me and the guy are getting it on.

"One by one the other guys will leave the table and come to the bedroom to watch. Then they will start asking if they can join in and I'll say "Maybe next time. I'll need a little time to prepare Bobby for it" and that will set up the next film in the series."

"And I get five hundred for just that?"

"And you will have to pretend to be cleaning me with your mouth when the fucking is done."

"Just pretend, right?"

"That's all, Herm, just pretend."

"When would this start?"

"Next week Tuesday if you say yes. I'll get together with you Monday and go over the script so that we can hit the ground running on Tuesday. When can you let me know yes or no?"

"Right now. Count me in. One thing though. This is all under the table, right? No taxes or any of that crap."

"You'll get the full five, Herm. In cash. Let's exchange phone numbers so we can stay in touch."

"I don't have a phone. You will just have to catch me here at the cafeteria," and I gave her my work schedule.

"Maybe when you get your first five hundred you can get a cell phone."

"I would like to know something."

"What?"

"Just who you were getting your information about me from?"

"You will see on Wednesday when you show up for filming."

"So I know him then?"

"Yes you do and I think you are going to be surprised."

"Why?"

"Think of every one you know and then try to figure out which one might be working in porn." She stood up and said, "I'll catch you Monday. See you then."

As she walked away I did what she said and tried to think of who I knew that might do porn films and I couldn't think of one. Then I smiled as I thought how many of them would have ever figured me for a male escort. Thinking of that took me back in time to a place where things had been a whole lot better.

***

I never knew my father. He caught the wind the day my mom told him that she was pregnant and she never saw him again. She went to work and raised me as a single mom.

We never wanted for anything. We had a nice home in a good part of town and mom always had a new or fairly new car. She traded her old one in every three years. She always had nice clothes to wear and so did I. She told me that she worked in an office as a personal assistant to the owner of the company.

I guess she didn't miss my father all that much, if at all, but she never married. She did date a lot, but I guess no one caught her fancy.

I was your typical kid. Ran around with my friends, played sports and chased girls. I was a better than average student and I lettered in football, baseball and basketball. Mom gave me a good allowance and life was good for me and the only bad spot was when my appendix ruptured and I ended up falling back a year in school.

The day after my eighteenth birthday, I found out what my mom did for a living. It was one of those spring days when spring fever grabbed you by the throat and knowing that mom wouldn't be home I skipped school and went home. I'd been there maybe an hour when the phone rang and without thinking "Hey, you aren't supposed to be here," I automatically answered it.

"Hello?"

"Is Jan there?"

"No she isn't."

"Who are you, her manager?"

"Her manager," I said and it was supposed to have come out as a question, but to the caller it must have sounded like a statement.

"This is Tony B and I need her for the day on Thursday. There will be two of us and Carl is really into anal sex. I know Jan charges extra for anal so make sure that she knows. Tell her nine at the Four Seasons in the restaurant. Whoa, I didn't ask. She is free for Thursday, right?"

"Yes, sir, she has nothing scheduled for Thursday," I said, not knowing if she did or didn't. He said goodbye and hung up.

I sat there as the call bounced around in my head. Mom charged extra for anal sex? That could only mean one thing. My mom was a prostitute! The next thought wasn't one of disgust, dismay or even disillusionment. I looked at the house and what we had and the new cars and thought:

"She is a prostitute, but she must be a damned good one to make the money that gave us the standard of living that we had."

I was no different from any other teenager with raging hormones. My mom was a sexy looking woman and I had accidently seen her naked a couple of times and the sight of her naked body had fueled many a masturbatory session and like a lot of other guys I'd even entertained the thought that I'd like to make love to my mother. The thought of my mom taking Carl in her ass gave me a raging hard on and I took my cock out and stared beating my meat as I imagined mom on her hands and knees sucking Tony B's cock while Carl was pumping her ass.

I was sitting there, eyes closed, imagining and whacking away when I heard:

"My God, Herman; what's gotten into you?"

I opened my eyes and saw my mom standing there looking at me. If it had been a minute or so earlier I would have dropped my cock and hastily tried to cover up, but I was a nano-second from getting my nut and there isn't a guy alive who doesn't know that at that time all that counts is the release. Your mind at that exact instant in time isn't all that clear either and it isn't working all that well. When I heard "What's gotten into you?"

I said without thinking, "You" and just as I said it I came and I'll swear that it went a foot straight up and then of course what goes up must come down and it did all over my lap.

My mom stood there looking at me stunned. "Me? You were doing that because of me?"

I still wasn't thinking clearly and I said, "You and Carl."

"Me and Carl? Who is Carl?"

By then my mind was starting to think a little more clearly. I realized that Tony B, whoever he was, would sooner or later talk to mom and she would find out about the phone call so I figured that I might as well tell her. When I was done she shook her head and I could see that she was about to cry.

"You were never supposed to know. Oh my God; you were never supposed to know. Whatever are you going to think of me now? And jerking off to an image of me and some guy named Carl who I don't even know. Oh my God!" And she ran off to her bedroom crying.

I cleaned up my mess and then headed to my room. As I passed mom's room I heard her still crying and, doing something that I had never done before, I went into her room without knocking. She looked so pitiful lying on the bed sobbing that I got on the bed with her, took her in my arms and held her. She cried into my shoulder until she was all cried out and fell asleep. I eased away from her, covered her up and went to my room.

***

The next morning mom was in the kitchen making breakfast when I got up. When I walked into the room she pointed at a chair and said "Sit!" I sat down and she said:

"I'm sorry that you found out about me. I never intended that you would know. Now that you do know, I have to make a couple of things perfectly clear to you. I am not ashamed of what I do. I've made a damned good living for us doing it. The second thing is that even though what I do may make you think less of me and lead you to believe I am someone with low or no morals, there are lines that I will not cross. Yesterday when I caught you doing yourself you told me that it was because of the image of me having sex. Get that thought out of your head. You can imagine having sex with me all you want, but it is never going to happen! You are my son and I love you to death, but not in that way. Never in that way! Are you clear on that?"

"Yes, ma'am."

"That out of the way, I supposed that you have some questions for me. Ask them and I'll do my best to answer them."

Of course I had questions. Why? When? How long had it been going on? I sat there and listened as she told me the story.

She was in love with Charlie Snyder and they were going steady. They were seniors in high school and Charlie had said he was going to marry her when they graduated. He convinced her that since they would be getting married anyway they could start making love immediately. Mom got pregnant, told Charlie and two weeks later he was gone and his parents wouldn't talk to her.

She finished high school, had me and my grandmother baby sat while mom found a job. I was a year old when my grandparents went to a party one night and they died in an accident on the way home. Grandpa got drunk at the party, ran a red light on the way home and got t-boned by a beer truck. There was just enough insurance to bury them. Mom couldn't afford to keep up the house payments and the bank foreclosed.

Next she lost her job, fell behind on her car payments and apartment rent and was a hair's breadth away from being evicted and having her car reposed when the apartment manager offered her a deal.

She could pay for the apartment with sex and he had friends who would pay well for a hot looking young chick. Mom was desperate so she took the deal. She did well at it and in a year she had paid off her car and had money in the bank.

One of her customers asked her to go to a party with him and she met a man there who knew what she was doing and asked her why a hot number like her was hooking out of her apartment instead of working as an escort and making much better money. He put her in touch with a man he knew who had an escort service and she went to work for him. In two years she had an established following and was constantly booked so when the owner of the service had a heart attack and died, she struck out on her own. She had more than enough repeat customers to maintain her standard of living and she was always getting referrals from her steady customers.

Mom told me that we were financially well off and that she had plenty of money set aside to pay for my college education. Then she asked if now that I knew what she did, did it change my view of her? I told her no, and that in fact all that it made me think of was that I could never be one of her customers. She gave me a funny look when I said that, but didn't say anything.

Nothing changed between us other than I was now aware of what she was doing when she was at work and that I wished I could also be doing. Not fucking her, but fucking. I was still a virgin and it didn't seem to matter how hard I tried I couldn't get rid of my cherry.

One night, about six months after mom told me her story, I was at home and horny. Mom was on 'a date' and I didn't expect her back for a couple of hours. I was sitting on the couch beating my meat when mom walked in on me. She looked at me, shook her head and said:

"I hope you aren't thinking of me while you are doing that."

The truth was that I was thinking of her. I'd never gotten the picture out of my mind of her that I had gotten after the phone call from Tony B. I still saw Carl pounding her ass while she sucked on Tony B and

I whipped off to it a couple of times a week. I knew it made mom uncomfortable thinking that I was jacking off to her so I lied and told her I was fantasizing about one of the cheerleaders at school.

She asked me why I jacked off so much and I told her that until I could finally get rid of my cherry that whacking off was my only sexual relief.

"You are still a virgin?"

"I'm afraid so."

"But why? You are a good looking young man and I was sure that you were getting plenty."

"Don't know, ma. I just can't seem to get a girl interested."

"I never would have guessed it. Well, we can't have that. We will just have to do something about that."

I smiled and waited for her to start taking off her clothes, but it didn't happen.

Two days later when I got home from school she sat me down and said:

"I'm going to ask you to do something that you are going to think is weird. I want you to go on a double date with me."

"A double date? I don't understand."

"I have a client who always comes to town with his wife. She goes off to find a sweetie for the night while Bob and I do our thing. They are coming to town and I want you to take care of Linda while I take care of Bob."

"You can't be serious."

"Of course I am. I've already talked to Linda and she knows that you are a virgin and she can't wait to get her hands on you."

A chance to lose the hated title of virgin? And it was set up by my mother? How hinkey was that! Of course I said yes.

"When?"

"Tomorrow night. We will meet them in the restaurant at the Hilton at six-thirty. Sports coat and tie. Okay?"

They were already there when we arrived. I was introduced to Bob and Linda, but not as mom's son. I was supposed to be the kid from next door who had the obvious hots for her, but she was too friendly with my parents to do me. Later Linda told me that mom said that I had confessed my virgin status and almost begged her to take my cherry. One night Linda had told my mom that she was tired of the hit or miss bar scene and she just wished she could find some hot young stud she could 'go steady with' when she was in town and that's when mom told her about me. Like I said, I found that out later.

As we were introduced I saw that Linda was about mom's age and that she was a sexy looking lady. I wondered why her husband wanted to fuck other women when his wife was to die for. Whatever, she was going to cure the malignant disease I had. You know, virginity.

We had a pleasant meal and mom and Linda chatted about girl type stuff while Bob and I talked sports. After coffee and dessert Linda said:

"You two have fun. Herm and I need to be going."

She stood up and offered me her hand. I looked at mom and she winked at me. I stood up, took Linda's hand and she led me to the elevators.

I can't even begin to describe the trip to paradise that Linda took me on that night. She had me undress her slowly and then she undressed me. She told me not to be embarrassed because the first couple of times would be quick, but my recovery time would also be quick. She went to her knees and sucked my cock and I'm embarrassed to say that I was indeed quick. She swallowed my output and as she stood she said:

"That got the first fast one out of the way. Now I'll show you how to return the favor when a girl does that for you."

She led me through how she liked her pussy eaten and cautioned me that other women might like it done differently, but what she was giving me was the basics.

"If you want to impress them, ask them what they would like and don't just munch down."

After several minutes of eating her pussy (and I will admit to some trepidation when she told me I had to eat her – guys didn't really do that, did they?) she said she was ready. I mounted her and then started slamming into her, but she stopped me and told me to slow down.

"Take it easy and go slow at first and then pick up speed after both of us are settled into a rhythm."

Again, I came too fast, but she told me not to worry and that it would get better. And thank God that it did. We went four times that night and the fourth time lasted almost fifteen minutes.

I met mom in the coffee shop at six and as we had breakfast she asked me how things had gone and I told her that I hadn't wanted to stop. She smiled at me and said:

"Maybe you won't have to."

"What does that mean?"

"We'll see."

When we got home mom handed me five one hundred dollar bills.

"What's this?"

"I don't do it for free, kiddo, and you aren't going to either."

"Five hundred for doing what I would have been willing to pay to do?"

"With any luck, sweetie, that won't be the last. Linda and Bob will be in town for another two days. I won't be seeing Bob again, but Linda wants to see you again on both days. Are your grades good enough that you can miss two days of school?"

I was wrung dry when Linda left town. She taught me cowgirl, reverse cowgirl, doggie and what she called the rear leg lift. We did anal and sixty-nine, but I balked when she wanted to try water sports. Luckily she didn't hold that against me. She spent a lot of time teaching me how to treat a woman properly and it was to stand me in good stead.

A week later mom asked me if I wanted to have a date that night and of course I said yes. Her name was Helen and she was close to fifty and I guess she was apparently happy with me because before the night was over she told me that she would be using me more often. I also found out from her that she thought that I was from an escort agency that she and her husband often used. I came to realize that my mom was the agency she was referring to.

From then on mom set me up on the average of once a week and I never got less than five hundred dollars for doing what I would happily done for free or even have paid for. I saw Linda on the average of once a month and once she even offered to set me up in an apartment to be her full time boy-toy and while I was sorely tempted I didn't want to move to Chicago.

***

Things went great for over a year and then disaster hit me. Mom was run down by a hit and run driver and died at the scene. So there I was at nineteen and a half still a senior in high school and orphaned. I had no other living relatives and I was totally on my own.

I had to make the arrangements for my mom's funeral and all of that. I didn't think I needed to worry about money because mom had led me to believe that we had plenty. She had told me that we had enough to carry me all the way to a PHD if that was what I wanted and the house was paid for, but when I started digging I couldn't find it.

I did find that she had set me up with a trust fund that would pay me five hundred thousand when I turned thirty, but there wasn't much else. She had thirty-two hundred in savings and eleven hundred in checking, but mom had no will that I could find so I ended up having to hire an attorney to get me access to her accounts. She had a ten thousand dollar life insurance policy in my name and it took all of that plus the four thousand that I had saved up to buy a car to pay for mom's burial expenses.

I thought that I'd come out okay because I would have mom's car, but that didn't work out either. I found out that she didn't buy a new car every three years – she leased cars. Mom's car had to go back to the dealership and I even owed some fees on it.

When the dust cleared I had my name on the house and six hundred in the bank. The lawyer's fees ate up what was in mom's checking and savings accounts. My career as a male escort was over because it had all come through mom. Basically I was stone broke. I was able to start college because I had scholarships and I was able to get a job in the student cafeteria that included my meals. I put the house up for sale, but because of the economy it wasn't moving.

Samantha's offer of five hundred for acting in her movies was a godsend.

***

Samantha caught me during my shift at the cafeteria and we arranged to meet Monday after I got off work. She handed me several pages stapled together and it wasn't quite what I expected. I was expecting a script that described each scene complete with dialog, but what I got was a description of what would be going on. The dialog was strictly ad lib according to the circumstances and situation.

"Is this it?" I asked.

"What did you expect? This isn't some Hollywood big budget epic. It's a fuck film and all that the people who are paying to watch it or buy it want to see is a sexy looking slut taking some dick. I try to make it look real instead of fake, but that's as far as I go."

She went on to explain what would happen and what I would be expected to do and say. My dialog was going to be "Yes, dear," "Whatever you say, dear" and "Whatever you want, dear." I was to say it with a hang-dog look and that I should try and make it look like even though I was agreeing I was hating it.

She ran through how the series was going to go and then she told me that if the series went as well as she hoped, she might add to it and I could have even more pay days if I wanted. She gave me an address and told me to be there by six and I told her I couldn't make it before six forty-five because my shift at the cafeteria wasn't over until six-thirty. She thought for a minute and then said that six forty-five would work.

When I got to the address I found that it was a private residence. I rang the bell and Samantha answered the door. She was wearing nylons, high heels and a bathrobe.

"Good. You are here and we are ready to shoot our first scene."

She led me into a large bedroom where there were several people and a couple of cameras set up.

"This is going to be different than what I told you about. The guy for what was supposed to be shot tonight had something come up and he couldn't make it. We will do his scene tomorrow and do the poker game tonight."

She took off the bathrobe and I got instant wood. She was incredible! Firm tits that stood out from her chest like the heads of torpedos and tipped with nipples that looked to be about an inch long. Her shaved pussy looked mouth-watering and I was immediately sorry that I wasn't going to be one of the guys fucking her.

"This is the last scene in the second of the series. Abe has just finished fucking me and I've called on you to do your duty and clean me out with your mouth."

There was a bowl of stuff on the dresser and as she picked up a turkey baster she said:

"This is a mixture of KY lotion, egg whites and cornstarch. It looks just like cum."

She filled the baster, lay down on the bed and put the baster inside her pussy and pumped the baster's contents into her. She pulled the baster out, handed it to one of the guys in the room and then squeezed her muscles until some of the stuff ran out of her. It did look like cum leaking out of her pussy.

"Ignore the cameras, Herm. Just pretend there is no one but the two of us here in this room. Can you do that?"

"No problem."

I could say that and mean it because I was used to having people watch me. Bob used to like watching me and Linda and in fact he did do a lot of what I was going to pretend to be doing with Samantha.

"We ready, guys? Roll them."

"Rolling," the two guys with the cameras said and then Samantha called out, "Get in here, Bobby," which was going to be my screen name. I walked up to the bed and Samantha smiled up at me.

"He fucked me good, Bobby. He came a lot. See?" she said as she spread her legs and pointed to the mixture running out of her. She dragged a finger through it and held the finger up to me. "Taste it, Bobby." I hesitated and she said, "I said taste it, Bobby," in a forceful tone. With obvious reluctance I bent my head, took her finger in my mouth and as I sucked it clean, Samantha said:

"That's a good boy. Now do your duty, Bobby."

I let go of her finger and stood there looking down at her. I made no move to do what she wanted.

"Don't make me ask you again, Bobby. You know what I expect. Now do it!"

"Yes, dear," I said as I got on the bed. Still I hesitated and she grabbed my head and pulled it down to her pussy and said:

"Eat, you little mother fucker, eat!"

I ate her pussy while the cameras moved in and got a close up of me slurping up the mixture. After two minutes or so Samantha said:

"Good boy, Bobby, but you didn't do it when I first told you to do it so no pussy for you this week. Now go and run a bath for me."

I stood up and said, "Yes, dear," and then one of the guys on the cameras called out, "Cut," and Samantha sat up and asked:

"How did it look?"

"Perfect," one of the camera guys said. "I don't know where you found him, but he is a natural at this."

"You been holding out on me, Herm? Have you done this before?"

I smiled at her and said, "A guy's got to have some secrets."

She gave me a long look and then said, "Okay, guys, let's move it to the dining room."

In the dining room the table was set up for cards and there were five guys sitting there talking. I was introduced to them as the cameras and lights were set up and then Samantha said:

"Okay, guys, let's make it look real."

I looked around the table and then said, "Same as always. Dollar, five and ten. Three raises, no check and raise and dealers choice. Pony up, gents."

The guys each gave me a hundred and I gave them poker chips and then we cut the cards for the deal. We played four hands, I won two of them, and then Samantha walked into the room in heels and a little black dress. I looked at her and asked:

"What are you doing here? I thought you were going out with the girls."

"Barb and Sue called and cancelled so I decided to stay home. I can play hostess. Any one need another beer?"

Every one said yes and she left the room and came back with six beers. As she set them down on the table the one named Abe said:

"Damn, Bonnie (her screen name), you look good enough to eat tonight."

"You guys are always saying garbage like that, but when it comes time to do it, you all run."

"Not this guy. When I say it I mean it."

"You any good at it?"

"I've never had any complaints."

"I guess we are going to have to find out if I'm going to be the first to have to do that. Come on; let's take it to the bedroom and see if all you are is a braggart or if you are telling the truth."

Everyone at the table looked at me and Samantha said, "Don't look at, Bobby. He won't mind. Right, Bobby?"

I tried to look dejected as I said, "No, dear."

The camera followed Bonnie and Abe as they headed for the bedroom and then cut back to me sitting there looking dejected. With my head down I said:

"My deal. Five card draw with jacks or better to open. Ante up."

As the guys threw in their chips I started dealing the cards. As the cards fell on the table one of the guys said:

"You let her get away with shit like that?"

I looked down and mumbled, "I can't stop her."

The guys picked up their cards and were looking at them when one of them said, "Fuck this shit! I gotta see this," and he threw in his hand and got up and headed for the bedroom. The other guys looked at each other, tossed in their cards and got up and followed him.

I watched them go and then said, "I guess I win," and I raked in the pot. One of the camera guys called out, "Cut." One of the camera guys came over to me and said:

"You have done this before, haven't you?"

It was a statement and not a question so I gave him an honest answer and said, "No."

"You sure can't prove it by what I've just seen."

The crew all moved to the bedroom and set up for the next scene. When things were set, one of the guys called out, "Ready to roll" and a few seconds later another of the camera men said, "Rolling." The cameras caught Abe and Bonnie walking into the bedroom. Abe moved to take Bonnie in his arms and kiss her, but she pushed him away and said:

"None of that. I only kiss Bobby."

"You only kiss Bobby, but you fuck other guys?"

"We aren't here to talk about Bobby."

She lifted her dress, pulled off her panties, laid down on the bed and spread her legs. Abe started to undress and Bonnie said:

"Don't bother with that. You don't need to take your clothes off to eat me."

Abe hesitated and it was clear that he had expected to fuck Bonnie, but with everyone crowding into the room to watch he had to back up his boast. He got down and went to work. I don't know if he was any good at what he was doing or Samantha was a great actress, but it sure looked like he was getting her off. After several minutes she gasped:

"Get your fucking clothes off. I need you in me. I need you in me now!"

Abe stripped in record time and was on the bed and in her in a flash. They fucked for a while and Samantha (or Bonnie if you prefer) moaned, clutched and grabbed. Then Abe pulled out of her, got her up on her hands and knees and rammed it to her. She got very vocal at that point and the room rang with:

"Fuck me! Goddamn you fuck me. Fuck meeeeeee."

The camera panned to the group standing just inside the door watching and one guy said, "God this is hot," and another one said, "She's hot. I want some," and a third guy said, "Think she'll do all of us?" and the fourth guy said, "We can ask."

The camera moved back to the bed where Abe was pounding away.

"Get ready, you hot little bitch. I'm going to pump you so full of it that it will come out your ears."

"Do it, damn you, do it!"

The camera moved up to Samantha's face and when it did Abe pulled out and came on the far side of Samantha's leg – the side away from the camera – and Samantha either had a real orgasm or faked a really good one. The camera panned over to the watching group. I wasn't supposed to be there – my part was done when the group left the table – but when the camera swung our way I lowered my head, looked sad and shook my head in a "How could you do this to me" way.

While the camera was on the group of watchers, a guy ran up to Samantha with the turkey baster and filled her up. The camera cut back and zoomed in on the ooze running out of her pussy. Samantha laughed and said:

"Looks like Bobby has a big wet spot to sleep on tonight."

One of the guys watching asked, "Can I be next?" and another guy said, "I want some too," and a third guy said "Hell, we all want some."

Samantha looked at them for a couple of seconds and then said, "Maybe next time. I'll have to prepare Bobby for something like that."

"Prepare? He's a fucking wimp. Just do it."

"He may be a wimp, but he's my wimp and if you expect to fuck his wife you had better be nice to him."

One of the cameramen, I found out later that his name was John and he was the chief cameraman, called out, "Cut" and the group started to disperse. Samantha sat up and said:

"How did it look?"

One of the camera guys said, "I've seen and shot a lot of porn in my time, but this is some of the best I've ever seen. We definitely have a winner here."

Then she noticed me and said, "You still here?"

"No way I could leave after seeing how hot you looked in your heels and that little black dress. Somewhere in this six film series you just have to fuck your poor hubby at least once."

"Ya think? We'll see. It is an idea with possibilities. Tomorrow, same time and place and tomorrow you will find out that your job has some fringe benefits."

"Benefits? Like what?"

"Wait and see. You will be surprised."

She told me the basic scenario for the next days' shoot and then I went home and with the image of Samantha in my mind I exercised my right hand – twice!

***

Samantha had been right. When I got to the house the next evening there were two other women there and I knew both of them from shared classes. Ivy and Fran smiled when they saw me and Ivy said:

"Am I forgiven for steering Sam to you?"

"You were the one?"

"Guilty."

"No wonder I could never get you to date me. I guess I'd seem a pretty tame guy to a porn star."

"I'm not a porn star. All I d…"

"I see you've met my two jewels," Samantha said as she walked up to us. "I told you last night that your job had benefits and this is them."

"Benefits?"

"You ever heard the term 'fluffer'?"

"Yes, as a matter of fact I have."

"Ivy and Fran are my fluffers. These two are the weirdest girls I know. They are both virgins and swear that they will walk down the aisle as pure as the driven snow, but they both love to suck cock. If you smile sweetly at them they will take care of you. You don't have time now though. We need to go over the scenario for tonight's shoot and then we will be ready for you to do your part.

"Tonight," Sam said, "my steady boyfriend will drop by for a visit. He has been here many times and he is familiar with the house and you. He will treat you like the wimp he thinks you are. Are you one of those 'manly men' or are you somewhat open minded?"

"I don't understand what you are asking."

"Okay. It will add a touch of realism to the scene tonight if my wimpy cuckold husband would take hold of Mike's cock and guide it into me. A 'manly man' would never be caught dead doing something like that, but a fairly opened minded guy might. It is something that a thoroughly cuckolded husband would do. What I'm asking is would you do it? You don't have to, but it would definitely add believability to the film if you would."

I thought about it and then said, "I'll do it, but there is a price."

"What?"

"I get to make love to you at least once before we are done. On film or not – at least once."

"You really think that I'm that hot?"

"We both know the answer to that and you also know damned well that you are."

She contemplated me for a couple of seconds and then said, "Deal! You know where the bedroom is."

As she walked away I looked at Ivy and said, "She's joking, right?"

Fran laughed and said, "Not a bit, Hermie, not one little bit."

I looked from one to the other, shook my head and then headed for the bedroom.

It was a repeat of the night before. The mixture and the turkey baster and then the:

"Get over here, Bobby. You know what to do. Do a really good job and I might change my mind about you not getting any pussy this week. Would you like that, Bobby? Would you like a chance to fuck your wife?"

"You know I would."

"Then get down there and clean me out."

"Yes, dear."

When it was over she said, "Very good, Bobby. You can have an hour on Saturday night. Make sure that you have condoms."

"You don't make the others wear condoms."

"If you want my pussy, Bobby, you WILL USE A CONDOM!"

"Yes, dear."

The next scene was me answering the door bell and letting in her steady boyfriend.

"What's up, Bobby," the man said when he walked in. "Here to fuck your wife again. You going to watch and cheer me on?"]

I gave him a nasty look and said, "She's in the kitchen," and then I walked away from him. As I walked away he said:

"Hey, ass wipe! It isn't my fault that you can't do the job and your wife has to come to me to get what she needs."

Without turning back around I gave him the finger as I walked away. He walked into the kitchen and a minute later Bonnie hollered out:

"Get in here, Bobby!"

I walked into the kitchen and Bonnie gave me a hard look and said, "Mike said you were disrespectful to him when you let him in. You know I won't stand for that. Now apologize to him."

I took a deep breath, looked down at the floor and said, "I'm sorry, Mike. I didn't mean to be disrespectful."

"Look him in the eye when you say that, Bobby."

"Yes, dear," and I repeated it while looking into Mike's face.

"Good boy, Bobby. Now go and turn down the bed and get the strappy high heels that Mike likes out of the closet. Then you can help me get ready."

I went into the bedroom and while the cameras set up, Ivy showed me the high heels I was supposed to get. When the guy on the camera said ready, I went out of the room and when he called out, "Rolling," I walked into the bedroom, turned down the bed and got the high heels out of the closet and set them on the bed.

Bonnie and Mike walked in. "Get me ready, Bobby," Bonnie said as she walked over to me. I slowly undressed her and when she was naked she sat down on the bed and said:

"Put my 'fuck me' shoes on me, Bobby."

I picked up her heels, put them on her feet and then buckled the straps. Bonnie got on her hands and knees and Mike walked up behind her with his stiff dick leading the way. Bonnie looked at me and smiled as she said:

"You know what to do, Bobby," and I walked over and took hold of Mike's cock with my left hand as Bonnie said, "Guide him into me, Bobby. Good boy," she said as Mike pushed into her. "Go sit in the chair, Bobby, and watch a real man fuck me."

I went over and sat down on the chair. After a couple of minutes watching the two on the bed I decided that it was time to do some adlibbing. The cameras were on the couple on the bed and I waved to get John's attention. When he looked over at me, I pointed at the tent in my pants and he smiled and nodded. The camera panned over to me and zoomed in on the obvious erection under my pants and then I surprised him and took it out and started jacking off while watching Mike fuck Bonnie. All the while two guys with regular cameras were walking around taking still pictures for the gallery portion of the porn site.

I make no excuses here. Samantha was one of the sexiest women I had ever laid eyes on and undressing her and putting her 'fuck me' shoes on her feet while staring at her shaved pussy got me going. Watching her tits sway as she turned her head from side to side sending her long hair swirling as Mike boned her had me hard as a rock.

After some footage of me sitting there and jacking off while watching my wife getting fucked, the camera swung back to the action on the bed. John motioned for me to leave the room and I put my cock away, got up and left. I found Fran and Ivy waiting for me. I watched as they did 'rock, paper and scissors' and Fran won. Fran went to her knees in front of me, took my cock out and then stared at it.

"My God, Herm, you should be in the other room being the star. How big is it?"

"One girl measured it and said she got twelve inches, but she measured from the base. From the top it only measures ten."

"It's just beautiful, Hermie," she said and then she took me in her mouth and started sucking me off.

Ivy was smiling at me and she said, "I'm next."

The thing with Bonnie had me so hot that I only lasted a couple of minutes and Fran swallowed every last drop I spit out. She pulled away letting my limp dick fall from her mouth and Ivy went to her knees in front of me and took my dead dick in her mouth and went to work to make it alive again. It was just starting to come up when I heard, "Cut," from the bedroom and then John's voice saying:

"Okay, guys, set up for the next shot. Herm, we need you back in here."

I hesitated and Ivy said, "Go. I'll be here waiting when you get back."

I went back into the bedroom and John, the head cameraman, pointed at the chair and I went over and sat down. John motioned for me to unzip and when I pulled out my half-hard cock he yelled:

"Ivy? We need you in here."

Ivy came into the room and saw what was needed and went to her knees in front of me. She captured my cock in her mouth and went back to working on it. It took several minutes, but she got me up and then left the room. John said:

"Do what you were doing, okay?"

I nodded a yes and started stroking myself. On the bed Bonnie and Mike had apparently gone from doggie to missionary while I was out of the room and as soon as I started beating my meat for the camera, it panned back to the bed where Mike was dicking Bonnie. Mike sped up and said:

"I'm coming, you hot sexy bitch," and Bonnie cried out, "Give it to me; give it to me and fill me up."

The camera came back to me still whipping away and while the camera was on me, Mike pulled out and Ivy dashed in with the turkey baster and filled Bonnie up. Mike pushed back into Bonnie and the camera went back to the couple on the bed. Mike pulled out and a bunch of fake cum oozed out of Bonnie's hole.

"Bobby," Bonnie said, "Be a dear and let loose of your thingy long enough to get us something to drink."

"Yes, dear," I said as I stood up and put my dick away. I left the room and Fran handed me two glasses of water. I waited a minute or so and then went back into the room and gave Mike and Bonnie their drinks. Bonnie said:

"Thank you, Bobby. You are just such a sweetie. Mike wants to do my ass next. Help me get ready for him, please?"

John called out, "Cut," and Bonnie got up from the bed. She gave me a funny look and then said:

"Why didn't you tell me that you were hung?"

"No need. You told me right at the start that I was only going to be playing a bit part and that I wouldn't be fucking you."

"I guess I did, didn't I. Oh well, a subject for later. This next scene you are going to use KY lotion and your thumb and fingers to get my butt ready for Mike. It will no doubt get you stiff so Ivy or Fran will take care of you when you are done."

She got back on the bed in the doggie position and John handed me the bottle of lotion. He said:

"Places, everyone. Okay. We are rolling."

"Come on, Bobby. Get me ready for Mike's big beautiful cock."

I moved up behind her and went to work on her butt hole. After a minute or so I decided to adlib again. While working on her butt hole with my right hand I used my left to unzip. I took out my cock and rubbed it against her ass-cheeks. She felt it and she let me continue while she decided on how she wanted to play it.

"God damn you, Bobby; get the fuck away from there. You know you can't have my ass."

In as whiney a voice as I could manage I said, "Why not, Bonnie? You let everybody else have it. I'm your husband so I should be able to have it too."

"We have had this talk before, Bobby, and you know full well why you can't have my ass. I'm upset with you, Bobby, and I'm going to have to punish you for trying something you know you are not supposed to do. You will sleep in the spare bedroom for the rest of the week. Maybe no snuggling and cuddling for a week will make you think twice before doing something like this again. Now get away from me. Maybe Mike can take my mind off of what you just tried to do."

I slunk out of the room and found Ivy waiting for me. "Ready for me?" she asked.

"You bet. It's a shame though."

"Why?"

"Because now I can't ever date you. I mean you never would say yes before, but I planned on keeping on asking. I can't do that now."

"Of course you can," she said just before she took my cock in her mouth. I've had head plenty of times and it was always good, but Ivy's blow job was damned near state of the art. She brought me to the edge and then backed off only to bring me back to the edge again. Finally I couldn't take it anymore and I grabbed her head and held it while I erupted.

She swallowed every bit of it and then licked my cock clean. She stood up and said:

"You want to date me, you have to kiss me. I mean right now."

I didn't understand what was going on, but I did want to date her so I took her in my arms and kissed her. She slipped me some tongue and I gave her some back. She broke the kiss and smiled at me.

"I know what you are thinking, Herm, and it is simple really. I'm a cocksucker and the taste of cum is always likely to be in my mouth. I make no excuses, Herm. I love sucking cock and I love the taste of cum and any guy who spends time with me is going to have to kiss me and that means that he is going to taste other men and he is going to have to be able to handle it."

"Why have you always said no when I tried to get a date?"

"Because dates are always trying to get in your pants and I won't let them. I could just suck them off, but before long I would have reputation and I don't want that. I know that would happen because that is what happened to me in high school. I haven't dated anyone since high school because I don't want it to happen to me here. Sam is a sorority sister and we roomed together during one term. She knows about my not giving up my cherry until I'm married and she knows how much I love to have a cock in my mouth so when she went into porn she brought me along as her fluffer. It gives me all the cock I could possibly want. Nights when they shoot gangbang scenes I've had the cum of as many as twelve men in my mouth. Now that you know that about me, you might not want to date me knowing that when you kiss me you might be tasting other men."

"I wanted to date you before finding out you suck cocks, so why, especially after finding out how good you are at it, wouldn't I want to date you now? You can always brush your teeth and gargle before we go out."

"That's the sticking point, Herm. I don't suck cock because I love throbbing meat in my mouth; I do it because I love the taste of sperm. I walk around all day savoring the taste of what's coating my mouth and I don't brush my teeth until the taste fades."

"No problem. We can time our dates so that you will have time for the taste to fade."

"You still aren't getting the picture, Herm. Sam has three porn sites up and running. This one you are in will be her fourth. She uses me on the average of four times a week. If we date there are bound to be times I haven't brushed my teeth or gargled. What I'm telling you is that if we date you will eventually be tasting some other guy's goo. That is why I said that any guy I date has got to be able to handle it."

"I still want to date you. I don't know if I can handle what you say I'll have to be able to handle until it happens."

Just then a call came from the bedroom. "We need you in here, Ivy."

She went into the room and John said, "We need to get Mike back up, sweetie."

Ivy went over to Mike and I saw that his cock was slick with the juices of him and Samantha. Ivy took him in her mouth and I remembered that Mike had been fucking Samantha in her ass when I left. I wondered if he came in Samantha's ass or had he pulled out, cleaned his cock and then went back to her pussy. While Ivy was working on Mike, Samantha walked over to me. Watching her sexy naked body walking toward me with cum or the turkey baster mixture running down her leg got me instantly hard again. When she got to me she said:

"I won't be needing you again until next Tuesday, but I'll want to get together with you again before then to go over how the rest of the series is going to go. What day would be good for you?"

"Any day except Thursday or Friday. Those are my late days at the cafeteria."

"Saturday good for you?"

"Any time after three-thirty. I'm at the cafeteria until three and then I'll need a half hour to clean up and change."

"How about I pick you up at your place around four?"

"It will work for me."

She went back into the bedroom and a couple of minutes later Ivy came out. "This would be a good time to see if you can handle kissing me while I have another man's juices in my mouth."

"No thanks, Ivy. When I left the room Mike was fucking Samantha in her ass. I might have been able to handle kissing you after your sucking a cock that came out of a pussy or that had cum in your mouth, but no way I'm kissing a mouth that sucked a cock that was just pulled out of a shitter."

She gave me a long look and then shrugged and said, "Whatever. Your loss. Get your fluffing from Fran from now on."

She walked away from me and I looked over at Fran who was sitting on the couch. She shrugged and said:

"If you want to date me, the same rules apply, but even though I will fluff a dick that's been in an ass I won't do it until it has been washed clean. And I will brush my teeth and rinse out my mouth before a date."

"Thank God for that. I guess I'm done until next week. See you at school."

Fran smiled and said, "I've got nothing going on for the rest of the week."

"That an invitation?"

"Bet your ass it is."

"How about we have lunch at the cafeteria tomorrow and talk about it?"

"Eleven-thirty good for you?"

"That will work fine."

***

"So how did you get involved with Sam?" I asked Fran.

"Ivy is a good friend of mine and she told me about what she was doing and I knew Sam so I told her that if she ever needed another girl to give me a call. I'm just like Ivy. I love the taste of sperm. I know I'll love the hell out of actual intercourse, but I made my mom a deathbed promise that I'll go into my wedding night a virgin and it is a promise that I'll keep."

"But if you promised to be a virgin, how did you find out that you like the taste of sperm?"

"Where I went to high school if a girl didn't put out she didn't get asked out very often. I found out that if I wanted to go out on dates I had to do something. I got real good at giving hand jobs and then one guy that I really, really liked talked me into giving head. I did, he came in my mouth and the rest is history. I never got a reputation because I only did it with guys who went steady with me and only after we had been going together for a while. Enough about me; what about you?"

"Nothing to tell. Just a guy working his way through school. Never knew my dad and my mom died in an accident last year. No other living relatives. Just a pretty dull guy."

"Hardly dull. There has to be more to you than that. You took to what Sam has you doing pretty easily."

"An older woman relieved me of my virginity and then taught me everything she could. She and her husband were a little on the kinky side and he liked to watch so I'm used to being seen in sexual situations and sometimes he even told me what he wanted me to do. It was almost like he was being a director at times."

"She taught you?"

I nodded a yes.

"She teach you to eat pussy?"

Again I nodded a yes.

"You any good at it?"

"She never complained."

"I guess then that the only question is when are we going out?"

"Any days except Thursday and Friday. Those are my late shift nights at the cafeteria. And of course I won't be able to on the nights I have to work for Samantha."

"That would only be on Tuesday and Wednesday. She edits the film and puts it together on Thursday and Friday so she can post them to her sites on Saturday."

"That leaves us Saturday, Sunday and Monday and I guess we could have a late date after I get off my shift at eight so which one do you want?"

"I'll take tonight."

It was a fun date. Fran had a very bubbly personality, she was easy to talk to and she was very, very easy on the eyes. We went to dinner and then took in a movie before I took her home with me. Once I saw Fran naked I was sorry that all I was going to get were blow jobs. Her blow jobs were great and I guessed that I could learn to get along with only head if Fran and I dated.

When I drove her home I kissed her goodnight and she slipped me some tongue and when we broke the kiss she asked me:

"Can we do this again?"

"As often as you want," I said and we made a date for Friday. It was a repeat of our first date and I decided that I could be very happy with just Fran's blow jobs.

***

Saturday Samantha picked me up at the house and drove us to the downtown Hilton. When I saw where we were going I thought of all the times I'd met Linda and all the other ladies my mom had set me up with at that very same place. Something must have shown on my face when I had that thought and Sam misread it.

"Don't sweat it, Herm. This is a business dinner and I'm picking up the tab."

When we were seated and after we had ordered, Sam asked, "So tell me, Herm; how do you like being in porn?"

"The money comes in very handy."

"You have impressed John and he wants to use more of you. I have three other sites up and running and I can always use fresh talent. When I saw the size of your package, I thought that maybe I could offer you more work. More active work if you know what I mean."

"What would that do to your cuck series? I'm guessing that your sites are linked so how is the viewer going to take my being a stud in one and a wuss in the other? Won't that kill the realistic feel that you are trying to get in the cuck series?"

"Well there is that, but after the cuck series has been up for a while I can use you in others and it shouldn't matter. That's something that we can come back to later. What I really wanted to talk with you about is the cuck series. Like I said, John is impressed with you and your instincts. Your doing the jack off thing was unexpected and added a lot to the feel of the film. Also your adlibs on the use of condoms and using my ass were just right for the situation.

"What I want to do tonight is give you an overview of the series and get your input as to what we can do to make it better. Also the more you know about what is coming, the more you can think about what to add to it if you do decide to do more adlibbing. Make sense?"

"It does."

"Okay, you already know the start. I did my boyfriend in front of you to establish that you are a wimpy and subservient husband. The poker game is the third in the series. We had to shoot it when we did because of the availability of the players. Number two in the series is Mike and a friend of his. Then the poker game. The fourth one will be me and a couple of guys I picked up on a girl's night out. After which I'll tell you that I have decided to do all the players at the next poker game. The fifth will be the poker game gangbang. There will only be you and four other players and Abe won't be one of them. At the end of the gangbang I'll say that it is too bad that there weren't a few more guys. One of the guys will say that he has a friend that likes to play poker and that Abe will be at the next game and then ask me if six will be enough and I'll say that it will do.

"The sixth is another poker game gangbang and Abe will have brought a friend so there will be seven and when it is all over and I'm laying there a fucked out mess, I'll look over at you sitting on the chair where I made you watch and I'll say something like you might as well come over Bobby and get some too. Then I might say something like "Just make sure that you put on a condom." You of course be upset because I'll be lying there with cum pouring out of me so why should you have to use a rubber. I'll say something like "If you want any pussy this week you will stop your whining and get over here."

"Then depending on how well the series is received, we may do a couple more to extend the series. That's what I have in mind. Do you have any ideas?"

"A couple. These guys at the poker game are obviously guys I work with or friends of some sort so it would be natural for one or two of them to take me aside and ask me why I put up what you do. I can say something like I love you, can't live without you and the only way I can keep you is by letting you have your way. Another would be for Bobby to get some pussy behind your back. It would be normal, at least to my mind, for Bobby, even though he is in love with you, to resent what you are doing and strike back even if you don't know he is doing it. Have him get laid some night after work and before the game starts so he comes home in a good mood. Then of course you will tear that mood down during and after the game."

"Those are good ideas and I think that we will use them to extend the series. How about you start an affair with a girl and after a while she, knowing what I do to you, decides she is going to take you away from me. She confronts me, we fight, I subdue her and then turn her against you and the both of us treat you like a servant. Another gangbang maybe with the two of lying next to each other on the bed as we take on the guys. Damn, Herm; I'm so glad that Ivy steered me to you."

She wiped her mouth with a napkin and said that she needed to use the ladies room. As soon as she was out of sight I felt a tap on my shoulder and a familiar voice said:

"How have you been, stranger?"

I turned and saw Linda standing there.

Chapter 2

Sam wiped her mouth with a napkin and said that she needed to use the ladies room. As soon as she was out of sight I felt a tap on my shoulder and a familiar voice said:

"How have you been stranger?"

I turned and saw Linda standing there.

"I don't want to intrude, but I do want to talk to you." She handed me a slip of paper and said, "My cell phone number. Call me, okay?"

"Tomorrow morning good?"

"Any time after nine."

She walked away just as Samantha came back.

"Who was the foxy lady?"

"A friend of my mother's. She saw me here and came over to say hello."

"I was afraid that she wanted to take you away from me tonight."

"Take me away from you?"

"I told you that I wanted to use you in some of my other films. Can't take fresh talent and put it to work without seeing how they perform. I took the liberty of reserving a room here for tonight. How about it, Herm? You ready for your audition?"

The woman flat wore me out. If it could be done we did it and some more than once. I thought Linda had taught me well. But Samantha taught me things that were probably against the law in some states. She would not quit until she could not get me up anymore. Talk about being rode hard and put up wet.

As we dressed Samantha said, "I definitely want to use you in some of my other films. Of course that assumes that you are interested."

"I'll have to think on it some. I'm not sure that I want to be a porn star. What I have done so far isn't going to make me noticeable. I'm more like background than anything else. But I do have to say that I could stand a steady diet of what we have just experienced."

"You weren't so bad yourself. Think on it. I really would like to use you in some of my other projects."

She dropped me at my house and I set the clock for eight and hit the sack.

***

I was up at eight, showered and dressed and on my way to my shift at the cafeteria at eight forty-five. My meals were a fringe of the job so I ate my breakfast and then looked at my watch and saw that it was ten after nine. I got up, cleared the table and then went in the back to use the phone to call Linda.

"Where have you been, baby? I've called and called and I have never been able to get in touch with Sarah. I've missed seeing you on my visits to your fair city. I'm here until Monday. Can I see you tonight?"

I saw my boss giving me impatient looks so I said, "I'm at work now and my boss is giving me nasty looks so I've got to hang up and get to work. Tonight? Same time and place?"

"I'll be the woman with the big smile on her face. See you there."

I was at the Hilton at seven and when I walked into the restaurant I saw her and she did indeed have a big smile on her face. When I got to the table I bent and kissed her cheek and then took the chair opposite her. She said:

"I thought that I would never see you again. I called and called and I could never reach Sarah. Why wouldn't she ever return my calls?"

Mom was gone so I figured that it wouldn't hurt to let Linda know the truth.

"Mom was killed and everything I did was set up through her. She didn't keep a client list so I had no way to get in touch with the ladies she set me up with."

"Your mom? Sarah was your mother? Oh wow! I'll bet there is one hell of a story behind that."

The waiter showed up at that point and we ordered and after he was gone I told Linda the story that had eventually led me to her.

"Wow! Your mom. I never would have guessed it. So what do you do with yourself now that you don't have all of us old ladies to play with?"

I told her about school and the job I had at the cafeteria. I didn't tell her about my gig with Samantha. Then she asked me what my major was and I told her that it was Business Management.

"How long have you got to go?"

"I'm in my junior year."

"What are your plans for when you graduate?"

"Find a job and get on with life."

Our order came and we made small talk while we ate. She asked me if I had a girlfriend and I told her no. She asked why not and I told her I couldn't afford one on what I made at the cafeteria. At the end of the meal and over Bailey's Irish Cream Linda said:

"I once offered to set you up in an apartment, but you said no."

"I didn't want to move to Chicago."

"What if I set you up in one here?"

"I don't need an apartment here. I'm still living in our house until I can sell it."

"How much are you asking for it?"

"Two hundred thousand."

"I'm not leaving until tomorrow. Any chance I could see it before I go?"

"If I'm right, you didn't ask me to be here tonight just for dinner so unless there is some reason that you need to use your room here, we can go to the house instead of your room."

"Let's do it."

When we left the Hilton I asked the doorman to get us a cab and Linda said:

"You don't have a car?"

"Can't afford one on student cafeteria wages. What I make is just enough to keep the gas and lights turned on at the house."

Linda told the door man to cancel the taxi and told me that we would take her car. We walked to the Hilton's parking garage and got in what looked like a brand new Escalade. I gave Linda directions to the house and she started the car and pulled out of the garage.

Once at the house I took her on a tour of the place. "You are only asking two hundred thousand? I would guess it to be worth around two forty."

"It was appraised at two thirty-six, but I priced it to move because I needed the money. I need a car and I still have a year and a half of school left to pay for and I would dearly love not having to work at the cafeteria. Unfortunately the housing market is flat right now and I've only had a half dozen people even look at it since I placed it on the market."

We were in mom's bedroom when Linda said, "You never gave me a direct answer when I asked you if I could set you up in an apartment. You just said that you had a house, but what if you sell it? Come on, Hermie; we both know what I am asking here."

As she was speaking she was unbuttoning her blouse and not being a dummy I immediately said:

"I know what you are asking and the answer is yes."

I was surprised that I was able to take care of Linda after the wringer that Samantha had put me through the night before, but she seemed satisfied when we fell asleep.

Linda woke me in the morning with a blowjob that led to a love making session that led to a joint shower which turned into another love making session. I didn't have much in the way of food in the house so Linda drove us to the Village Inn. After we ordered she said:

"Here is the deal. I come to town every other week. I usually get in on Thursday night, take care of business on Friday and then spend the weekend getting my needs met and then fly out on Monday morning. I'd want you available from seven p.m. on Thursday until I leave on Monday. Sound okay to you?"

I nodded a yes.

"Instead of setting you up in an apartment I'm going to buy your house."

"You can't be serious."

"Of course I am, Hermie. My company is an investment company and I see this house as a good investment. I pay two hundred for it and use it instead of the Hilton and that alone saves me fifteen hundred a month. When the market turns, and it will, I'll sell for what the house is appraised for. In addition I'll have my weekends covered. Sound good to you?"

"I'd have to be an idiot to say no."

"There is more. My car sets in the Hilton garage when I'm not here. You can use it and park it in your garage. You will need it to pick me up at the airport when I fly in and take me to the airport when I leave. I'll hire a maid service to come in once a week and I'll stock the pantry so I don't have to eat all my meals in a restaurant. That's what I will do. You already know what your part will be. Do we have a deal?"

"If you are really serious, I'm in."

"Good. Give me the name of your real estate agent and I'll get the ball rolling as soon as I get back to Chicago. The rest of the deal starts now. You drive me to the airport and keep the car until the next time I come back which will be the week after next. Do you have a cell phone?"

"I can't afford one."

"You can now," she said as she opened her purse and handed me five one hundred dollar bills and a business card.

"Get a phone – a good one – and then call me with the number. I'll need to keep in touch with you. Unless you have any questions I need to be headed for the airport."

"I'm sure that I'll think of several, but none occurs to me right now."

On the way to the airport I said, "I imagine that you and Bob will use mom's bedroom for yourselves. Anything you want me to do to get it ready?"

"Oh God; I'm sorry, I didn't tell you. Bob had a heart attack and passed away eight months ago. It will be just you and me in the room. It will be your room when I'm not here and our room when I am. One thing I am going to do is order a king size bed for that room. I don't know how Sarah could stand to sleep on that water bed. It has to go."

I dropped Linda off at the Delta departure area and headed back to town. As I drove I thought on how my life had changed in just twenty-four hours. It seemed to be too good to be true so I was going to treat it that way. I wouldn't be giving up my cafeteria job until the deal on the house went through. I didn't doubt that Linda meant what she said since she had given me the keys to the Escalade, but the impression I got was that Linda was a very busy lady and might not get to it right away. She might get busy and not even remember about it until it was time for her next visit.

***

I had two classes that morning and then a four hour shift at the cafeteria followed by two more classes and so it was five-thirty before I got to the AT&T store on Fourth Street. I bought a phone and then called the number on the card that Linda had given me. My call went to voice mail so I left a message with my new phone number and went on home.

Now that I knew I wouldn't have to be moving anytime soon, I decided to start moving from my room into mom's bedroom. It was twice the size of my bedroom and had its own bathroom. Before I could move in though, I needed to get the full size waterbed out of the room. I set it up to drain and got the process started.

While it was draining I started cleaning out mom's walk in closet and bagging all of her clothes to give to Goodwill. I was putting the last of her shoes into a bag when my new cell phone made the noise that passed for ringing. I answered with a "Hello?" and heard Linda say:

"Hi, baby. Miss me?"

"You know I do."

"Just calling to tell you to call your realtor and give him your new phone number so he can reach you. My manager of Acquisitions will be calling him tomorrow. Also I need to know when you will be home so I can set up the delivery of the new bed and when you can be there so the girl from Merry Maids can look over the place. You will also need to get a couple of keys made. One for the maid service and one for me."

"Just give them my phone number and have them call me."

"I have a dinner meeting that I need to get to so I'll talk to you later."

So much for my thinking that she wouldn't get to buying the house right away. The bed was still draining so I went to make myself a sandwich and as I was spreading the Mayo it occurred to me that I should call Samantha and give her my number. As soon as she heard my voice she said:

"I hope you aren't calling to cancel on me. I need you, Herm. The response from the first video has been fantastic and I have over four hundred emails asking for more. I've never gotten a hundred on any of the other stuff I've put up on my sites."

"No fear, dear lady. After Saturday night I've got to hope and pray for more and that means that I have to stay on the good side of you. I'm just calling to let you know I now have a cell phone and to give you the number."

"Good. That will make things easier. Tomorrow at seven? Same place."

"I'll be there."

By the time I finished my sandwich the mattress had drained so I wrestled it out into the garage and went back to the bedroom and started to take the rest of the bed apart. I'd put it up on Craig's List and see if I could make a couple of bucks on the deal and if I couldn't I could always give it to Goodwill or put it out on trash pickup day.

When I lifted the plywood up off the slats, I saw a gray metal box and I wondered what was in it and how mom got access to it. It would have been a huge pain to try and lift the mattress and plywood to get at it and then I mentally smacked myself for being so stupid. No way would she do that. I bent down and took a close look at the bed skirting. There were what I thought were carved decorative panels along the length of the base and the one in front of the box popped out when I pulled on the edges.

I picked up the box and opened it. It was packed full of hundred dollar bills and there was also a key chain with a key on it. I counted the money and it came to $118,600 dollars. I wondered why mom hadn't put it in the bank and then I realized that she couldn't. That much money would have raised questions about where it had come from and I'm sure that mom wouldn't have wanted people to know what she had done to earn it. Also if she didn't want to pay taxes on it she wouldn't want to put it in a bank. I wondered about the key and it then occurred to me that it might be a key to a safe deposit box.

I set the box on top of the dresser and finished taking the bed apart and moving it out to the garage with all thoughts of selling it gone. I didn't need the money anymore so I would give Goodwill a call. I took six hundred out of the box and then put it in the bottom drawer of my dresser underneath my socks and underwear.

***

I had Tuesday off at the cafeteria so after my last class I drove downtown to the bank where my mom had kept her accounts. I asked for Mr. Byrns who was the man who had handled things when mom died and I had to get access to her accounts. He confirmed that the key was to one of their deposit boxes and since he has been the one the attorney had dealt with, he knew I had a legal right to access the box. He turned me over to a woman who took me to the room where the boxes were and then she left me in private.

I opened the box and found more money. A quick count showed that there was over $106,000 dollars in the box and there were also several gold coins and a number of small gold bars. I had no idea what gold was worth, but with the box I had found under the bed I now had almost a half a million dollars and I still had $200,000 coming from the sale of the house. Talk about a sudden turn around in circumstances! I put everything back in the box and then treated myself to a steak dinner before going to meet Samantha.

***

When I got to Samantha's she said, "Tonight we will shoot the episode where Mike brings over a friend. We will start out with you eating me after the two men finish with me. I've made a change in the way we are going to shoot the actual threesome scene. They are going to ridicule you and I'm going to lay there smiling as they do it. Then one of them will say something about you not being man enough or maybe not having a dick big enough to satisfy a woman like me.

"I'll tell them that I treat you like shit because you are mine and I can, but I have to draw a line on how others treat you so I will tell you to drop your pants and show your package which is bigger than Mike's or his friends. Then I'll call you over to me and take you in my mouth and then say that you taste better too."

She was silent for a moment and then said, "No. Never mind the taste thing. I'll do that the night I pick up the two men at the bar. Do you think you can do the cock insert thing tonight?"

"I did it before and it didn't kill me."

"I'll want you to prep my ass for one of them. We good to go?"

"Can do."

We shot the scene where I had to suck to goop out of her and then we shot my opening the door and letting Mike and his friend in. I did put Mike's cock in her and I prepped her ass for the guy playing Mike's friend and I even guided him into her. Then I went and let Fran take care of my hard on. I got nasty looks from Ivy, but I ignored her.

Then Fran and Ivy had to get to work on getting Mike and Ralph (the guy playing Mike's friend) up again so they could finish the shoot. While that was going on I went and saw Samantha to give her the bad news.

"I'm not going to do any more after the cuck series. I've finally got a buyer for the house and I'm not going to need the money."

"You are going to stay with me until we finish the series, right? I mean even if it goes beyond the original six episodes?"

"I'll stay until the end. I have an idea for the girl's night out episode."

"What is it?"

"I assume that you have other female actors?"

"I do."

"Bring one of them home with you from the girl's night out. Her and maybe three guys instead of two. She does one while you do the other two. She finishes hers and wants more. She sees me leave the room and while you aren't looking she follows me out to where I'm sitting on the couch. She tries to seduce me and I fight it and make a big speech on how I can't cheat on you."

"Okay, but how about this. She listens to your speech, but then gets aggressive. You put up token resistance and she gets your cock out and starts sucking it. You let her get away with it for a while before getting up and rushing out of the room. We can use it to set up your affair. Your thinking will be that if Mimi could get you up and into doing it even after your speech some other girl could do it also, but you would have to do it away from the house where I wouldn't know about it. Then you rationalize it believing that the only reason you ran away from Mimi is because you were afraid I would come into the room and catch you."

"That will work."

"I don't need you any more tonight, but see if you can come over an hour or so earlier tomorrow. I have some things I want to talk to you about, but right now I have to get back to work. The envelope on the dresser has your five hundred for this week in it."

I got the envelope and on my way out I asked Fran if she was doing anything Friday and she said she wasn't so I asked her out and she said yes. We set a time and I left.

***

The next day after my first two classes I went to the cafeteria and gave them a week's notice. They weren't upset because it happened all the time as a student's circumstances changed. Also they had a waiting list of students who needed financial aid.

I was on my way to my next class when my phone rang. I answered it and it was Tony from Empire Realty.

"I've got an offer on your house and it is for the full asking price."

"All I've got to say is when do we close?"

I had to turn the phone off before going into my next class and I forgot to turn it back on until I was on my way home after my last class. I had two missed messages and a voice mail. I listened to the voicemail first and it was from a furniture store wanting to set up a delivery date. They were also one of the missed messages. I called and set up a time for them to make their delivery on Thursday. I called the other missed message and found that it was from Merry Maids and I set up a time to meet their representative at the same time as the furniture delivery.

Wednesday after my classes and my cafeteria shift I went over to Samantha's place and got there about an hour and a half early. She greeted me in a bathrobe and I could see that she had on high heels and nylons. When the door closed behind me I heard her say "Herm?" and I turned and saw that the bathrobe was on the floor.

"I don't have anything to talk to you about, Herm. I just want to ask you for something."

"What?"

"I want you to make love to me. I don't want to be fucked. I want to be treated the way you treated me Saturday night. Please, Herm? Make love to me?"

I was going to say no?

As we got dressed and got ready for the crew to arrive I just had to ask:

"What just happened here?"

"I told you. I'm paying my way to my doctorate by fucking on film, but that's all I ever get is fucked. I'm just a piece of meat to the actors and I'm no different from most other women in that I want some tenderness, some sort of emotional connection. I got that from you our first time and I wanted more."

Just then we heard "Anyone home?" from the front room. The crew had started to arrive. I got another surprise that night. The girl who was going to be the one who came home with Sam from her girl's night out was Diane who was a girl who was in two classes with me. I had asked her out several times and she had always politely turned me down. She was as surprised to see me as I was to see her. I wondered how many of my other classmates Sam had on her payroll.

The first scene was done very quickly. Bonnie told me that she was going out for the evening with her girlfriends.

"I probably won't be coming home alone so don't go to bed early. I might need you."

"Yes, dear," I said and the scene was over.

The next scene was me sucking the goo out of Bonnie after she had fucked the three guys that had come home with her. I was getting used to the mixture from the turkey baster, but it was never going to become a favorite of mine. The next scene was the five of them coming home from the night out and then the five of them undressing. When Bonnie was naked she told me to:

"Come over here, Bobby, and get me ready for Rod."

"Yes, dear," I said as I knelt and licked her pussy for a minute and then she said:

"Put him in me, Bobby, and go sit in your chair."

I did it and then sat on the chair as Bonnie and Mimi (Diane's film name) and the three guys played on the bed. Watching did get me hard and I got John's attention and pointed at my crotch. He got the message and the camera swung toward me as I took out my cock and started to beat my meat.

Bonnie was doing two and the third guy was doing Mimi. The two guys on Bonnie came and when they got off of her she said:

"That was nice, wasn't it, Bobby? Did you like watching?"

"Yes, dear."

"Be a good boy, Bobby, and get us some refreshments. I'll have a white wine and I suppose Mimi will want one also and you can get the men some beers."

She put emphasis on the words 'boy' and 'men' and I meekly said, "Whatever you wish, dear," and I left the bedroom. I came back with a tray that had two glasses of wine and three bottles of Pabst Blue Ribbon on it. The five finished their drinks and then Bonnie started sucking one guy and another moved behind her and started taking her doggie. Mimi was trying to get the third guy up, but the camera angle made it look like he wasn't responding.

I left the room and went into the living room and sat down on the couch. The crew came in and started setting up and while they were doing that Sam was explaining to Diane what was supposed to happen in the scene. John looked at me and asked if I was ready and I nodded a yes and he called out, "Rolling."

Mimi, still naked, came into the room and sat down next to me. She reached over and ran her hand across the bulge in my pants and said:

"My guy left me hanging, baby. Can you help me out?"

"Help you? How?"

"You've got a stiffy under those pants, honey, and I've got a nice warm place you can put it."

"You mean have sex with you?"

"Good idea, huh?"

"Oh no; I couldn't do that. I can't cheat on Bonnie."

"Get serious! She's in the next room cheating on you wholesale and you are telling me that you can't do a little of what she is doing? She is married to you and fucking other guys, honey, and that is called cheating."

"But it isn't cheating. It is her way of testing my love for her. Letting her do what she wants without complaint shows her how much I love her."

"So she should let you do what she does so you can see how much she loves you right?"

"Oh no. She told me that if I really love her I'll never look at another woman."

"So don't look at me, honey. Just close your eyes and I'll do the rest."

She pulled my zipper down and reached in for my cock, but I pushed her away and said:

"No! I can't!" and I got up and rushed out of the room. Just as I cleared the doorway I heard John call out "Cut!"

I went back into the room and John came up to me and said, "Sam tells me that you are bailing out on us."

"Not until the series is done."

"You won't reconsider?"

"I might. I just don't know. I only got involved because I need money, but I've just come into some and I don't need the work anymore."

"I hope you change your mind. You are a natural and have a feel for it. Got some damned good ideas too."

Diane came up to me and said, "I saw you sitting on the chair whacking off. It looked good to me. Will I ever get the chance to try it?"

"I've asked you out a half dozen times over the last year and a half, but you have always said no."

"That was then. You are part of my life now. I hold myself to only dating guys I work with. I love sex and if I didn't hold only to guys I work with and who I know are not going to be running around blabbing about me I'd have a reputation that no girl in her right mind would want. So what do you say?"

"Can I have a rain check? Right now I have so much going on that I don't know what nights I'm going to have free."

"Just keep me in mind, sugar."

"I will. I promise."

And I would, but I'd already committed to Fran for Friday and I was hoping that Friday would lead to Saturday, but then I thought with Fran I'd only be getting blow jobs. With Diane I would be able to get some pussy. I asked her for her phone number and she gave it to me.

The next scene was the poker night gangbang and it went pretty much like the first like the first gangbang, but with a few differences. We did the usual eat out Bonnie after her being fucked scene and then as we did the card playing scene the guys talked about how hot my wife was and how lucky I was to have a babe like that.

About five hands into the game one of the guys asked where Bonnie was and I muttered:

"In the bedroom."

"Why is she there? She should be getting us some beers."

Just then Bonnie walked into the room wearing a bathrobe. "You want beers?" she asked. "I thought I'd offer you a different kind of refreshment," and she let the robe fall to the floor and stood there naked except for her high heels. I got a stricken look on my face and said:

"Please, Bonnie, don't…"

"Stop whining, Bobby! You keep whining and I'll start getting the idea that you don't love me anymore. Deal each man a card, Bobby. High man goes first and the rest in the order of their cards."

I sat there staring at her until she snapped, "Do it, Bobby!"

I kept my head down as I dealt the cards.

"Hot damn!" one of the players exclaimed. "An ace and I thought I wasn't lucky at cards."

He got up and Bonnie led him into the bedroom. After a minute all the other guys got up and went into the bedroom to watch.

There was a short break while the crew set up in the bedroom. One of the cameras stayed on me and after everyone had followed Bonnie into the bedroom she came back alone and said:

"I'm going to need you in the bedroom, Bobby."

"Why are you doing this to me, Bonnie? I work with these guys and I have to face them every day."

"Get in the damned bedroom, Bobby, or you won't be getting any pussy for a month."

She turned and headed for the bedroom and when she was out of the room I muttered:

"Maybe not from you."

I stared at the door for a minute and said out loud to myself, "I'm beginning to wonder if you love me at all," and then I got up and followed her into the bedroom.

All the guys were naked and Bonnie said to me, "A couple of these guys aren't sure that you are okay with this, Bobby. Show them that it is all right with you."

"How?"

"You know how, Bobby. Just do it."

I stood there and stared at her until she said, "Don't you love me anymore, Bobby?"

I swallowed and then walked over to the guy who had drawn the ace and who was standing by Bonnie. I took a deep breath and then took his cock and guided it into Bonnie. Once he was in her and stroking Bonnie told me to go sit in my chair until she needed me to do something. I did as I was told only this time I didn't take my dick out. I just sat there and tried to have an unhappy look on my face.

The first guy finished and then the second one took his place. Halfway through the second guy's turn another guy said:

"She can do more than one. How about we make her airtight."

He and another guy went over and the three men arranged Bonnie so she had a cock in her ass, cunt and mouth. The guy in her pussy finished, got off her and another guy immediately took his place. The guy who had just finished went into the other room where the first guy who had fucked Bonnie was being fluffed by Ivy. He sat down on the couch and Fran moved in to work him back up again.

On the bed the three guys were busy banging Bonnie's three holes and I decided to try and do some play acting and I sat on my chair and tried to look like I was crying. Trying to fake crying isn't easy, but I think I managed to at least look like it was what I was feeling.

The five guys rotated between Bonnie, Fran and Ivy for the next hour and then we wrapped for the night. Sam asked me if I had any plans for Saturday and I told her no.

"Care to have dinner with me? Maybe a few drinks and some dancing?

"I'd like that."

"Meet me at the Hilton?"

"No. I'll pick you up here at seven."

"I thought you didn't have a car."

"I do now."

"Okay. Seven it is."

***

Thursday my last class was at two so I was home by four. At five the furniture company arrived with the new bed and a matching dresser and vanity table. While they were carrying them into the house two women from Merry Maids showed up and I took them on a tour through the house. After they had looked over everything they told me that they would be doing the house every Wednesday and one of them took a list out of her purse and went looking through the kitchen cupboards. She saw the curious look on my face and said:

"I've got a list of what Mrs. Baxton wants in the way of groceries and I'm looking to see if you have any of it so I don't have to buy it."

After everyone was gone I went up to the bedroom and set things up the way I thought Linda would want it and then I went and worked on my homework until it was time for bed.

Friday I worked my last shift at the cafeteria and when classes were over I went home and dressed for my date with Fran. I picked her up at seven and we had dinner and then went to the Brass Rail which was a country/western bar and had a great time there until the place closed.

In the parking lot before I even got the car started Fran was next to me and was pulling my zipper down. I decided to just sit there and enjoy it rather than get a hum job while driving. The girl did know how to please a man with her mouth. When I took her home we made another date for Sunday night.

Saturday I did yard work around the house until it was time to get ready for my date with Sam. I picked her up and we went to Duke's Steak House for dinner. I intended to take her dancing, but when I asked her where she would like to go she said:

"To bed."

"To bed?"

"I can't help it, baby; I like making love with you."

"Okay then; to bed it is."

I drove to the house and we went inside. Sam looked around and said:

"Very nice. Do you think we might be able to shoot the episode where you cheat on me here?"

"I guess we could."

"Where is the bedroom?"

"In a hurry?"

"Damned right I am."

I took her upstairs and just before I was going to take her into the master bedroom I had the sudden thought that I shouldn't. Linda had purchased that king sized bed and she should be the first person to make love on it so I steered Sam into what used to be my room. Sam noticed and asked why we hadn't gone into that room.

"That's Linda's room."

"Who is Linda?"

"Tell you later. Right now I can't wait to see that little black dress hit the floor."

I slowly undressed her and then she sat on the edge of the bed and watched as I undressed. When I was naked she laid back, smiled and waited for me to join her. We made slow easy love three times before snuggling up together and falling asleep.

In the morning after a shower that followed some early morning love making Sam asked:

"Okay, so who is Linda?"

I explained Linda to her and she looked at me incredulously. "You are a male escort?"

"Used to be, but not anymore. Starting next week I'll be a kept boy toy."

"I can't believe it. It is just too wild."

I shrugged and asked, "Where would you like to have breakfast?"

"Some place close so we can hurry back. I'm not done with you yet. An escort; oh wow."

Over breakfast she pumped me for the story and I told her how it all started.

"Your own mother was your pimp?"

"I guess you could call her that, but it was more like she was the owner of an escort service."

Then she wanted to know how many women I'd slept with as an escort and when I told her around fifty she exclaimed:

"Om my god. No wonder you were so at ease doing porn with me. So this Linda got your cherry?"

"She did."

"And she was the one who taught you how to take care of a woman?"

"Indeed she was."

"If I ever meet her I've got to remember to thank her."

We finished eating and then went back to the house where Sam insisted that I show her more of what Linda had taught me. It was a thoroughly exhausted Herman who took Sam home that night. I walked her to her door and she kissed me. The kiss turned passionate and she led me inside where I wasn't as exhausted as I thought I was. I fell asleep cuddled up to Sam and slept like a dead man.

In the morning I got an oral wake up that led to us playing most of the day. It wasn't until I was almost home that I remembered that I was supposed to have taken Fran out that night. I thought of calling her and telling her some story that might get me off the hook, but then I realized that she and Sam talked and Sam might just mention our date. I decided on telling a half truth and I called Fran and told her that I'd been in a meeting with Sam over the series and we had gotten so into the planning that I'd forgotten the time. I promised to make it up to her later.

***

Monday I was home from class around three and I sat down at the kitchen table to work on a paper I had to turn in for my Strategic Management class. At four forty-five my phone made the weird sound that passed for ringing and it was Linda.

"Hi, lover; miss me?"

"You know I do."

"Just touching base with you. I'm going to be very busy the next couple of days and may not be able to get back to you so I thought I'd give you a heads up now. My flight gets in at six-forty on Thursday. You can park in the waiting area and I'll call you as soon as I have my bags. Pick me up at the United arrival area okay?"

"Will do."

"This is a hell of a time to bring it up, but it never occurred to me to ask before. I know you said no when I asked you if you had a girlfriend, but who was that lovely lady I saw you with at the Hilton?"

"Samantha? I guess you could call her my boss."

"Really? What kind of work are you doing for her?"

What the hell, I thought, she knows I was basically a male prostitute so why not tell her so I did.

"Oh dear. Can you get out of it?"

"I suppose I could, but why?"

"Because I have plans for you, baby. When you graduate I want to bring you into my company. In fact I was going to offer you a summer internship in my office there."

"So why would that make me want to leave Sam?"

"Because you will be dealing with the public and someone who watches that stuff might recognize you and that wouldn't be good for your business reputation."

"The damage is already done. I've already made five and they have been aired. Besides, I have promised Sam I would stay to the end of the series."

"Try to get out of it, baby. Limit the damage."

"I don't think I can do that, Linda. I gave Sam my word and I always stand behind my word."

"I've got to go, baby. We can talk some more on Thursday. Looking forward to seeing, lover. Bye."

As I closed the phone I thought about it. Was risking a job working for Linda worth my going back on my word? I knew the answer before I finished the thought. No it wasn't. A man's word has to be worth something if he was to have any self-respect at all.

The phone rang again at six-twenty and it was Sam wanting to know if I'd eaten yet and when I said no she invited me over to her place.

"I made spaghetti and as usual I made more than I can eat by myself. Besides, I want to talk about the next two episodes."

"What time?"

"As soon as you can get here."

Twenty minutes later I was sitting at Sam's kitchen table eating spaghetti with meat sauce and garlic bread and as we ate we talked about the cuckold series. The next was going to be an eight man gangbang instead of the seven that had been originally planned. Sam had gotten some emails from subscribers asking if she was a racist because none of the actors in her films were black so two of the studs in the gangbang episode were going to be black.

What was going to be different than the poker game gangbang is that there wasn't going to be a poker game. It was going to be set up by phone by Abe who was going to call, say he had heard about what happened at the last game and ask her if she would like to do another one with a few more guys.

"Can you think of a way to make it work as far as the image of you is concerned?"

I'd given her my word that I would stay with her until the series ended, but that didn't mean that I couldn't try to end it sooner. I bit the bullet and told Sam about my conversation with Linda.

"I promised you that I would stay until the finish, but I see Linda's point about how it could affect my career in her business. I would like to end the series with just two more episodes after the gang bang."

"You don't have to do any more at all, Herm. I see where she is coming from and she is right. If your career is going to be dealing with the public you should do what she said and limit your exposure."

"I know, but I can't go back on my promise to you. I want to finish the series, but I'd like to suggest a few changes."

"Okay; let's hear them. Your instincts have been good so far."

"Use the gangbang to set up the episode where I cheat on you. I'll overhear you talking to Abe and you will disparage me. Call me a wimp and say you only put up with me because it turns you on to fuck over me. Say something like, "If I could find a real man I'd move him in and kick Bobby out on his ass.""

"We can do a split screen thing so both sides of the conversation can be seen and heard. Abe might say something like, "I thought you loved him" and you will say, "I don't love him I just love fucking over his wimpy ass." I chop up a bunch of onions so that when the camera cuts to me I'll be crying. I'll suck it up and not let you know that I overheard you."

"When we do the gangbang I'll refuse to do some of the things you'll tell me to do and then you will snarl at me and tell me to get out of the room and say something like:

"Get used to using your hand. It will be a long, long time before you get any more of my pussy."

"The next episode will be shot at my house and will all be me and another girl. We will make it look like it has been going on for a while. The bedroom at the end of the hall is set up as a home office and we can make it look like a work place. We can set it up so I'm talking to one of the girls I work with about a date and then we can set my patio up to look like an outdoor café where the girl and I have lunch. Over lunch I tell her my woes and have it go from there.

"We do the sex scenes at my place and make it look like the girl and I have gotten it on several times – changes of clothes and things like that- and that will set up my confrontation with Bonnie. The last episode will be the confrontation. If we do it right the series will end with me looking like I have a set of balls. That way if while working for Linda I ever deal with someone who has seen the series they won't think of me as a hopeless wimp."

"Sounds good. We can make it work. Speaking of making things work, would you like your dessert here on the kitchen table or in the bedroom?"

"Silly girl. The bedroom of course. If I had it on the kitchen table it would just be a fuck and you and I don't do that. Right?"

"Oh you are a silver tongued devil, aren't you?"

I ended up spending the night and waking up snuggled up to Sam felt real nice. I had to make a mad dash to my place to get my books and then rush to make my first class, but I did feel that it was worth it.

***

Tuesday the first thing we did was shoot the scene where Bonnie talked to Abe. It went pretty much as Sam and I had talked about. She shot me through the grease and the camera cut to me where I was standing and listening to the phone call. Because of what I had done with the onion I did have real tears running down my cheeks.

The next shot was me answering the doorbell and letting Abe and his two black friends in.

"Hi, Bobby," Abe cheerfully said. "Meet Jason and Terrell. Bonnie asked us to stop by. Where is she?"

"In the kitchen," I said in a tone that left no doubt about how I was feeling.

"You are okay with this, right?"

'Oh yeah, Abe; it just makes my day," and I walked off and left them there.

The next two scenes were me answering the doorbell to let the other players in and then a scene where Bonnie called me into the kitchen.

"Fix the drinks for our guests, Bobby, while I go and get ready for them."

"Yes, dear."

While I was making the drinks Terrell came up to me and said, "You are sure one fucked up white boy to put up with this shit."

I looked at him, shrugged and said, "You are just so right."

I handed everyone their drinks and then left the room. The next scene was Bonnie calling me into the bedroom and saying:

"A couple of these guys are pretty big, Bobby, and I know you don't want me to hurt so loosen me up down there. Eat my pussy and get me ready for them."

I ate her pussy for a couple of minutes and then she pushed me away and told me to go sit in my chair. I got up and walked right by the chair and out of the room.

"Bobby!! You get back in here. Now!! Right now, Bobby! Get your ass on that chair!"

I turned around and went back in and sat on the chair and did my best to look sullen. On the bed Bonnie had a cock in her pussy, a cock in her mouth and she had her eyes on me. As she sucked and fucked she winked at me and I just sneered and sat there.

The guy fucking Bonnie came and the guy in her mouth moved down to sink his hard cock into her pussy. While the movements were taking place Bonnie said:

"See how real men handle a woman, Bobbie? Don't you wish you could do it?"

I said nothing and just sat there and stared at her. About twenty minutes later when one of the black guys moved up to take his turn with her, Bonnie said:

"I want him in my ass, Bobby. Come over here and get me ready for him."

I went to the dresser and got the KY and went over and started working my thumb and fingers into her butthole. While I was doing that she was sucking Abe's dick and I decided to do some ad-libbing. I quietly pulled down my zipper with my left hand while my right stayed busy working on her ass. I got my hard cock out and then before anyone knew what was happening I leaned forward and pushed my cock into Bonnie's ass.

My ad-lib movement registered and Bonnie took her mouth off of Abe's cock and yelled:

"God damn you, Bobby! You know you aren't supposed to do that to me. Get off me, Bobby! You hear me, Bobby! You get off me right now!"

I reluctantly pulled out of her as I said, "At least now I can say I've been there."

"Get your ass on that chair, you little shit. You are going to pay for that little stunt."

I moved back to my chair with a smile on my face and sat on my chair and watched the rest of the gangbang. The men were dressing to leave as one of the black guys finished fucking her and when he pulled out Bonnie said:

"Get your ass over here and clean me out, Bobby."

I got up from my chair and walked over to her as she spread her legs wide. When I got to her I ad-libbed again and said:

"You know that chocolate gives me hives," and I walked by her and out of the room.

Bonnie yelled, "Get your ass back in here, Bobby. Right now or I'll make you sorry that you were ever born."

I didn't go back and she yelled, "You hear me, Bobby? Get your worthless ass back in here right now," and then I heard John call out, "Cut!"

Fran was taking care of my hard on when John came into the room and asked:

"What happened in there? What happened to the happy wimp?"

Fran hummed away as I said, "Didn't Sam tell you about the change to end the series?"

"Not a word."

"You need to get with her."

I felt my knees start to go weak and I said, "Excuse me, but I have something I have to take care of right now," and grabbed Fran's head with both hands and held it as my cock pulsed into her waiting mouth. I felt her mouth and throat movements as she swallowed and when my cock was limp she let it fall out of her mouth and then she stood up and kissed me.

"I hope that you noticed that I made an exception for you." I must have looked confused by what she said and she went on:

"I once told you that a cock coming out of an ass had to be washed before I would suck it and before I would kiss someone."

I hadn't given it any thought, but she was right. I had been in Sam's ass and hadn't washed my cock before Fran sucked it and she had kissed me when she finished.

"Why?" I asked.

"Why what?"

"Why did you do it?"

"You are becoming special to me, Herm, and I wanted to see if I was special enough to you that you would overlook it."

"If you hadn't told me I doubt that I would have even given it a thought. What do you mean when you say I'm becoming special to you?"

"Oh come on, Herm; you can't possibly be that dense. I feel that there could be something between us. You are the first guy I have ever been with that I've thought about making the long haul with."

I didn't know what to say to that. I liked Fran, but not in that way and how do you tell that to a girl when she is giving you some pretty damned good blow jobs. I decided that the easiest way out was for me to lie.

"I thought you knew I am engaged to be married?"

"Then why are you always trying to date girls?"

"Sandy goes to UCLA in California and we both like sex so we have an understanding. We are each free to play around until she graduates and comes back here."

I saw disappointment register on Fran's face and she turned and walked away.

"Is that true?" I heard from behind me and I turned and saw Sam standing there.

"No, but it was easier telling her that than to tell her I wasn't interested in being her special guy."

"Why not? She is a pretty sexy looking lady. She's smart and when she gets her degree she is going to do well in her field. Those are pretty good things to have in a woman and there is the plus that she is obviously interested in you."

"I admit that there is all that, but there is also an insurmountable obstacle in the way."

"And that is?"

"She made a promise to her mom that she intends to keep. I understand that, but I can't buy into it."

"What does that mean?"

"I will not marry a woman unless I know we are sexually compatible and that means that the woman I marry isn't going to be a virgin when she walks down the aisle. I may be a bit young to be such a cynic, but I have seen several marriages crater because of sexual issues. A lot of my clients back in the day were survivors of such marriages."

"So tell her that."

"Can't. What if she decides to throw away her promise to her mother and we just don't click? No; I think it best not to start anything."

Sam shrugged and then said, "We need to talk about the shoot tomorrow. Stick around and we can talk after everyone leaves."

I picked up a magazine from the coffee table and read it until everyone was gone and I heard Sam say:

"I really don't want to talk about tomorrow's shoot."

I looked up to see her standing in the doorway naked except for a pair of 'come fuck me' heels.

"I don't know how you feel about being the last man to ride the train, but I did douche and brush my teeth. I need what you give me, Hermie. Especially tonight. I've never felt more like a piece of meat than I do tonight. I need some loving, baby; not some fucking."

As she held out her hand to me I stood up and took it and she led me to the bedroom. It was another morning where I had to make a mad dash to get to my classes on time.

***

Wednesday night the shoot took place at my house and I met Shayna. Shayna was going to play the part of Celia who was the girl I would have my affair with.

We shot several scenes that looked like we were at work talking. Celia was supposed to be my secretary who had a crush on me. There were a couple of scenes to establish that we had a work relationship and once we had those we moved on to other scenes.

In one scene she came into the office and found me sitting at my desk crying and she rushed over to put her arms around me and comfort me. She wanted to know what was wrong and I broke down and told her about Bonnie and what she was doing to me.

"That bitch!! You need to get rid of that slut and get someone who will love you and appreciate you."

There were a couple of scenes shot on my patio which had been made to look like a sidewalk café and in one of those scenes Celia said:

"The next time she pulls that crap you leave and come over to my place. You don't have to stay there and put up with that shit."

I had a three car garage and we put three cars in it and filmed from an angle that made it like a parking structure in the city and Celia and I sat in the Escalade and did some heavy necking. The evening was spent setting up and filming Celia and I making love and when we were done and people were leaving Sam stuck around and when everyone was gone she just looked at me and said:

"Please?"

"Okay, but it will only be once. Linda will be here tomorrow and I need to be able to take care of her."

"You sound like you have feeling for her."

"I do. She is one hell of a lady and I owe her a lot."

"I do too. Owe her a lot I mean. I'm serious. I want to meet the woman that built you. Come on, baby; take me to bed."

***

Thursday I cut my last class so I could make it to the airport on time to pick up Linda. On the drive home I told her that she had an admirer that she'd never met.

"You have to explain that to me."

I told her about what Sam had said.

"Really? She wants to meet me? I think I'd like to meet her. I've never met a porn star. Invite her to join us for dinner Sunday."

"Are you serious?"

"Of course I am."

"Okay. I'll call her and see if she will come."

We talked about the cleaning service and the job they did on Wednesday. I told Linda that I couldn't find any fault in what they did.

"But what do I know. I'm a guy and house cleaning isn't something that I'm up on. They did bring in a lot of groceries which brings up the question of have you eaten yet? Should we stop some place?"

"No. If they stocked the place like I asked them to there should be the makings for a small salad. Will that work for you?"

"As long as there is Bleu Cheese dressing."

"There should be. That is my favorite also and it was on the list I gave them."

I told her about the scenes we shot at the house and how Sam agreed with her about limiting my exposure and I told her why I wanted to stay with the series and how I wanted to finish it.

"The damage was already done in the episodes that have already aired. If I finish the series the way Sam and I agreed on it might mitigate some of the damage and I'll come out of it looking like a stud with some balls."

"Silly boy. You are a stud and I'm rather fond of your balls."

When we got to the house Linda whipped us up a small salad and when we finished eating Linda asked:

"Is it too early for dessert?"

As we headed for the bedroom she asked, "Did I guess right on the new mattress? It isn't too hard or too soft, is it?"

"I don't know."

"What do you mean you don't know?"

"I've not slept on it yet. You bought it so I have been waiting for you to break it in."

She gave me a funny look and said, "I never knew that about you."

"Knew what about me?"

"That you had a sensitive side when it came to things like that. That is just so sweet of you."

Break it in we did and I'm surprised that we didn't break it while we were breaking it in. It was two in the morning before I finally fell into an exhausted sleep and as I faded away Linda was still trying to get me up again.

I didn't really want to get up in the morning, but Reynolds was notorious for hitting the class with pop quizzes and they accounted for twenty percent of your grade so I forced myself out of bed.

Linda was already up and in the kitchen. "Coffees ready and the French toast will be ready in about five minutes. Sleep okay?"

"Like the dead. Explain to me if you can how a woman your age can take a man my age – I'm supposed to be in my prime after all – and reduce him to a worn out husk."

"Easy. Mine doesn't quit and shrink like yours does."

She handed me a couple of pills and said, "Here; take these."

"What are they?"

"Vitamins. You need them. Last night was just the preview of coming attractions. What are your plans for the weekend?"

"Didn't make any. I kept it open for you."

"In that case I think we will stay in. Don't forget to call your lady friend and invite her over."

"My lady friend?"

"The one who wants to thank me."

"Oh. You mean Sam."

"I'll drop you off at school since I'm going to need the car all day. I probably won't get in until about seven or so. Rest up, lover; you are going to have a busy night ahead of you."

I knew that Sam had a ten o'clock in Harris Hall so I was waiting for her outside the classroom door when she got there. I told her that Linda wanted her to come to dinner on Saturday and she was surprised, but said that she wouldn't miss it for the world. I told her six and she said she would be there and then she kissed me.

"Why did you do that?"

"A couple of clowns in the class keep hitting on me. They are looking at us right now so I just let them know that I'm already taken."

"Already taken?"

"They won't know any different. Just play along."

I took her in my arms and gave her a passionate kiss and when I broke the kiss she gave me a look I couldn't decipher and then turned and went into her class.

I had dinner ready when Linda came in at a quarter to seven. It was just scalloped potatoes and ham with green beans, but Linda behaved like it came from a four star restaurant.

"I'm not used to a man who can cook. Bob, bless his heart, could barely boil the water he made his tea with."

"Mom insisted that I learn to cook. She felt that I might never get married to a girl who could cook and that I'd end up starving to death."

We ate and then as soon as the dirty dishes were in the dishwasher she said:

"Okay, lover; you know what I want for dessert."

It was another exhausting night and thankfully I didn't have to get up for class in the morning. Linda had a morning meeting that she had to go to so while she was gone I worked on a paper that was due in on the coming Tuesday until four-thirty and then I started dinner. Linda got home at five and asked me what I was doing and when I told her she told me that she had planned on fixing dinner.

"I didn't know what time you were going to get home and I told Sam dinner at six. You can do the cooking next time."

"We have time for a quickie?"

"When have we ever done it quickly? Non-stop is how I remember it."

"Poor baby. I'll take it easy on you."

We had just finished showering and getting dressed when the doorbell rang. I answered it and Sam took one look at me, grinned and said:

"I know what you were doing."

I blushed and stepped aside to let her in as Linda came up to us. I introduced them and we all walked toward the kitchen with the two of them talking like they were friends who hadn't seen each other in a while.

When we got to the kitchen Linda asked me how soon dinner would be ready and I told her about a half an hour.

"Fine. That gives you time to run to the store and get a nice red wine to go with dinner. Maybe a Merlot or a Cabernet Sauvignon."

She asked Samantha if she was a wine drinker and Sam said she was so Linda said:

"Maybe you should get two or three bottles."

I said okay and left. I wasn't dumb and I knew the wine thing was just something to get me out of the house so the girls could talk. As I drove to the store I wondered about that conversation, but guessed that I'd never know what was discussed.

When I got back to the house with six bottles of wine I found the two of them in my home office on the computer. They were watching Samantha's "I Make My Husband a Cuckold." They were watching the latest gangbang episode that Sam had either put up Friday or Saturday. I'd never pulled up the website so I'd never seen any of the episodes, but then

I wasn't really interested in seeing them anyway. As I walked into the room Linda was saying:

"That looks wild. I've never done anything like that. I wonder if I would like it."

"Want to try it?" Sam asked. "I could set it up for you."

"The idea does turn me on, but I don't know if I could actually do it. The kinkiest I've ever been is to do Herman while my husband watched and told us what he wanted to see us do."

"Well I do have to admit that gangbangs are not for everyone, but if you ever want to try just let me know and I'll make it happen."

Sam noticed me and said, "What do you think, Herm? Want to see your lady pull a train?"

"Not really."

"Why not?" Linda asked. "Don't you think I could do it?"

"No doubt in my mind that you could do it; I just wouldn't want to watch."

"Why not?"

"Because I'd want to ride the train; not watch it go by."

Linda laughed and said, "You nasty boy you."

"Me nasty? I'm not the one thinking of doing a gangbang. Come on you two; dinner is ready."

Over dinner the conversation was general in nature and covered topics like what Linda did and what Sam's plans were when she finished school. I don't know why it came as a surprise to me when Samantha said:

"Find a job in the field of my studies, find a good man and start making babies."

"What about your company?" I asked.

"My company?"

"Your adult entertainment company."

"I don't have a company. It is just me. You don't need to be a company to put up a website and post things to it."

"So what happens when you stop making films?"

"I shut it down or sell it to someone. It isn't as though it is my life's work. I only do it because I make enough money off of it to support myself and put me through school. PhDs don't come cheap."

Then Linda asked, "What are you looking for in a husband?"

"Someone with an open mind. He will have to know about what I've done to get me through school and be able to handle it."

"Why tell him?"

"Because sooner or later he would find out about all of the porn I've done and if he wasn't the right kind of guy we would end up in a divorce. Knowing up front and accepting it before saying "I do" will prevent a ton of problems."

"What are the odds on finding a man like that?"

"Pretty good. I think I have already found him."

"You have? Tell us about him."

"I can't just yet. I think he is the perfect man, but I need to find out a little more about him before I'm sure."

The talk switched to Linda's company and what she had in mind for me. Linda said she didn't yet know exactly where she was going to put me.

"Herm still has a bit of school yet and things could change between now and when he graduates. Where I'm going to put him will depend on where the economy is when he is ready to go to work." She turned to me and asked, "You are going to intern with me over your summer break, aren't you?"

"I don't know. I'm seriously considering taking a full load over the summer so I can move up my graduation date."

"I can understand that," Linda said. "But I think you would get more out of interning in the office so that when you come on board you would already be up to speed on the place."

"Maybe. I still haven't made up my mind. I've only recently come into the financial shape that will allow me to take summer classes."

After dinner we polished off another bottle of the Cabernet and talked until Sam looked at her watch and said that she had to be going. She and Linda exchanged hugs and cheek kisses and I walked Sam out to her car.

"I like her. Can I see you Monday?"

"Sure. What time?"

"I'll have dinner ready by seven, but you can come early if you like. You can always have dessert before dinner."

She kissed me again, got in her car and drove off.

When I got back in the house Linda said, "I guess I'm going to have to start looking for a new stud."

"Why would you say that?"

"Because I already know who Sam's perfect man is."

"Who?"

"You. She was looking right at you when she laid out what her perfect man had to be like. I could tell from the way she looked at you all night that she has you in her sights. You are the target lover. Women know about these things and you can trust me on that."

"I doubt it. She is a couple of years older than me and besides, she hasn't shown any interest in me other than I fit the profile of what she needed for the cuckold series."

"Trust me, lover; that girl has you down as her intended when it comes time to mail out the wedding invitations, but until then I still have you. Ready for an early turn in?"

As Linda and I made love I wondered if she was right. Was Sam thinking of me as her ideal husband? No. I just couldn't see it. I did have the right mindset as far as accepting what she was doing to pay her way through life, but me as a husband? Nah! I couldn't see it. Linda was dead wrong on that.

We were in bed until nine on Sunday. After making leisurely morning love we got up and Linda fixed us breakfast. Linda wanted to see the Museum of Modern Art so we spent the afternoon there, stopped at Griego's for dinner and drinks and then headed for home. Linda's flight was at six so we went to bed early, made love twice and then fell asleep cuddled up next to each other.

There was a moment of awkwardness when we reached the airport and Linda gave me an envelope with cash in it for my 'weekend services' and I wouldn't take it.

"I'm living rent free in your house and eating groceries that you stocked the place with and I'm driving your car all the time you aren't here. That's enough for me."

"It is still your house, Herm. We haven't closed yet."

"I'm not going to quibble with you, Linda. Keep the envelope."

She looked at me without speaking for a few moments and then she leaned forward and kissed me.

"See you in two weeks, lover," and she got out of the car. A porter took her bags and she waved just before disappearing into the terminal.

Chapter 3

I'd had a thought over the weekend concerning the money I'd found under mom's bed. Figuring that some people are just naturally nosy and if the cleaning crew that came in every Wednesday had someone like that, I'd best move the money.

Just before leaving to take Linda to the airport I stuffed what was in the metal box into a backpack. After dropping Linda at the airport I headed for a different bank other than the one where mom had her safe deposit box and opened checking and savings accounts and rented a deposit box. I'd move money from the box to the accounts a little at a time so as not to draw any attention. Over time I'd move the money from mom's original box to the new box. I felt relieved as I left the bank and headed for my first class.

I rang Sam's doorbell at six-ten and she greeted me wearing high heels and an apron.

"Just in case you wanted dessert first," is what she said as I entered the house.

I pulled her into my arms and kissed her and said, "I'll have dessert after dinner, but I think I will have an appetizer before dinner," and I picked her up and carried her into the bedroom. It was the start of another long night and Tuesday was another day when I had to race to make it to my first class on time.

Tuesday evening was a very tiring experience for me. I had to shoot three different scenes making love to Celia. The first time was on the desk in the home office and was shot so it looked like we were making love at work. The next two were in the bedroom on the queen size bed. There was a quick clothing change between scenes so it would look it was happening on different days.

Making love to Celia was hard work. There was concern on Sam and John's part that I wouldn't be able to fuck three times in a couple of hours so they had me stop every time I got close to getting my nut and someone would run in and do the turkey baster thing. Believe me it is hard – damned hard – to quit just before you are ready to cum. Sam and John's strategy backfired on them. The third time Celia and I made love I was so ready that I came a minute after I slid into her.

Then the call went out for a fluffer and that was another trip. Fran had taken the day off and so Ivy had to do the fluffing and she was not at all happy about it, but she had to suck it up (pun intended) and do her job. It took her a while before I got up again and got the shoot over with.

Sam wanted to stick around after everyone left, but I was too exhausted to do her any good and I told her so. She understood.

"Making love under the hot lights isn't as easy as it looks," she said. "But I know that you can use a good morning wake up so I'll stay if you don't mind."

Her good morning wake up consisted of waking me with a blow job and then leaning against the shower wall while I took her from behind. She gave me a passionate kiss before I hurried off to get to class and as I went out the door she told me that she would see me that night.

***

That night I was sandbagged!

The way it was supposed to work was that Celia, after falling in love with me, was going to confront Bonnie. They would get into a cat fight, Bonnie would subdue Celia and turn Celia into her bitch and then they would both laugh at me. I would make an impassioned speech about how I wasn't going to put up with Bonnie's shit any longer, tell her she was welcome to Celia, that I would be seeing an attorney first thing in the morning and then walk away.

In previous scenes we had established that Celia and I were falling in love and that we would both tell Bonnie that I was leaving her for Celia. Celia wanted to drive the message home so we decided that the confrontation would take place when Bonnie came home and found Celia and I making love on Bonnie's bed.

Celia and I made love only this time I didn't have to stop and pull out. I came in her, went soft, pulled out and then fell next to her on the bed. She reached for my cock and was playing with it when Bonnie came into the room. She took in the scene and then yelled:

"What the hell is going on here?"

"I knew from what Bobby told me that you were a stupid bitch, but I never thought you were so stupid that you couldn't figure out what you were looking at."

"Who the fuck are you?"

"I'm the woman who is going to take your husband away from you and treat him like the treasure he is."

"Over my dead body!" Bonnie exclaimed.

"My pleasure," Celia said as she jumped off the bed and went for Bonnie. The two put on a pretty good show, but then instead of Bonnie subduing Celia per the script I thought we were following, Celia got Bonnie down on the floor in a hammerlock and said:

"You want more, bitch? All I have to do is add a little more pressure and something is going to break."

"Enough! Enough! Stop hurting me."

Celia got up leaving Bonnie on the floor and then said to me, "Get dressed, Bobby, and let's get out of here. You can come back for the rest of your things later."

We both dressed and were heading for the door when Bonnie cried out:

"Don't leave me, Bobby; please don't leave me. I love you, Bobby; please don't go."

I had no idea why Sam had made the changes, but I did know that the episode was supposed to end with me showing some balls so I ad-libbed.

"You don't love me, Bonnie, and I doubt that you ever did. What you loved was shitting all over me knowing that I would take it because I loved you and didn't want to lose you."

"No, Bobby; you're wrong. I only did what I did because I thought it was what you wanted. If you would have ever told me to stop it I would have done it in a heartbeat."

"Bullshit, Bonnie. No way you could have believed that I wanted to be humiliated and shamed in front of my friends and the people I work with. And if you truly loved me there isn't any way that you could constantly deny me that which you gave freely to everyone else.

"I overheard your conversation with Abe the other day. I heard you tell him that if you could ever find a real man you would put me out on the curb with the rest of the garbage on trash pickup day.

"I loved you, Bonnie, and you will never find anyone who will love you more than I did, but you killed that love. You drove a stake through it and killed it and I'm out of here."

I took Celia by the arm and walked out of the room as Bonnie cried out:

"Please, Bobby; please. Please don't leave me."

I heard John call, "Cut and that's a wrap," and I turned and walked back into the room.

"What happened here, Sam?"

"The series ends without you in it so I decided to change the ending just a little. This way you showed that you had some stones and you got the girl. A happy ending for you. We can always reshoot it the other way if you want."

"No; I'm cool with it. I was just curious."

"Another reason is that it leaves open the possibility of your coming back if circumstances change. We can play it that you loved me so much you couldn't stay away. I'll be all sweetness and light, but gradually I'll get you back under my thumb. The difference will be that you are only a wimp with me. We can have you punch out a couple of guys to show that you are not a wuss except for me."

"Not likely, Sam. Linda was pretty definite in her wanting me to quit and I have to agree with her thinking."

"I do too. I would have stopped when you first told me about it."

"I know, but I promised you I'd stay through the series and to me a promise made is a promise kept."

"The series ends with this episode, but I do hope I'm going to see you from time to time."

I remembered what Linda said and I decided to be a little bold.

"My mom was forever telling me about a woman's intuition and that 'women know these things' and I've gotten the same from Linda;

especially the 'women know these things' bit. Just before she left to go back to Chicago she asked me if she was going to have to look for a new stud when she comes back to town. When I asked her why she told me that she 'just knew, just immediately knew,' that when you were talking about your perfect mate you were talking about me. I told her she was crazy and she gave me the 'women know' speech. Was she right?"

Sam was silent for a bit and then she said, "Would it be so bad if she were right?"

"You mean she was right?"

"She sure was. Right on the money, baby."

"But why me? You could have your pick of guys who would kill to have a woman like you."

"I already told you. I need someone who will accept me for not only who I am, but also for what I was. I can accept you knowing that you were a male prostitute and I believe with that background you can accept me. Am I wrong?"

"No, but what about love? I like you, Sam; I like you a lot, but I don't know that I love you."

"Bullshit, Herman! If you can make love to me the way you have been doing, you can love me. I already know that I've fallen in love with you."

"I don't know what to say."

"Don't say anything, baby. We will just take it as it comes. You know my schedule and what nights I can date. I'm betting by the time I finish my program and have my degree you and I will be what is called 'an item' in some circles and once I have that degree I am done with porn. I will be ready to live a normal life and I want to live that life with a guy who treats me the way that you do. Let's just play it by ear, okay?"

No way was I going to say no. Sam was a superior bed buddy; she was smart, witty, and I did like her a hell of a lot. I knew I could do worse – a lot worse – in picking a mate for life so I said:

"Okay, Sam; one day at a time."

***

Over the next two months I dated Sam between Linda's visits and we got along fine. I closed on the house and put the money in the bank. I had a year to do something with it to avoid paying capital gains on it.

Linda invited Sam over every time she was in town and the two of them talked about as if I wasn't even there. Sam told Linda she was going to marry me as soon as she got her degree and Linda asked me if it was true and I just shrugged my shoulders. Sam laughed and said:

"He just hasn't gotten used to the idea yet."

Every time the two of them got together they talked about gangbangs and I was beginning to think that Linda was actually going to do it.

Summer break came and I decided to work for Linda's company rather than take summer classes. The work was interesting and I got a lot of real world experience to compliment the classes I was taking for my major.

Sam and I got together two or three nights a week and at least one of those nights ended up in a sleep-over at either Sam's place or mine. Sam was done with her degree program and all she had left to do was submit her dissertation and defend it. I picked her up one Saturday and she told me she could see me every night of the week from then on.

"I posted my last film this morning. I'm all yours now, lover."

That night's sleep-over lasted until Thursday and I do have to admit that waking up next to Sam every morning was something that I could get used to in a hurry. That night I picked Linda up at the airport and she asked me if I had missed her and I said:

"You know I have."

"Really? Sam hasn't been keeping you too busy to even think of me when I'm not here?"

"I do spend a lot of time with Sam, but you are never far from my thoughts."

"That's a sweet thing to say, but I know that my time with you is short. Sam is determined to marry you and now that school is over for her she is going to put on a full court press. The two of you are perfect for each other."

"The problem is that even though I like her a lot I don't know that I love her."

"So what? There are more people out there than you realize who weren't really in love when they married, but love grew between them. Bob and I weren't in love when we married. It was a marriage of convenience, but by the time he died I would have killed for the man. You and Sam have unique backgrounds that make you the perfect couple. I know it and Sam does too.

"Let me put your mind to rest on something. You dumping this old broad to marry Sam isn't going to change my plans for you. I'm still going to expect you to come to work for me."

"What's with this 'old broad' crap? You are one hell of a sexy lady and what surprises me most is that you are wasting your time on some dude like me when you could have your pick of dozens of men who would like to put a ring on your finger."

"The problem is that most of those men who want to put a ring on my finger want to do it more for my money than me. Oh I'm sure that there are some who would want me for me, but do you have any idea of how many I would have to wade through to find those guys? And what happens if I choose wrong? No thanks, lover; I'll stick to you young dudes. You have fast recovery powers. More to the point I'll stick with you as long as you will have me."

"As long as I'll have you? I've got news for you, sexy lady. I'm yours until you tell me goodbye. I won't be the one who ends what we have."

"Oh? And what about Sam?"

"To be bluntly honest, Linda; I can't choose between you. I want you both."

"Oh dear; this could get sticky."

She was silent the rest of the way home. When we got there Linda helped me make dinner and after we ate we sat on the patio and sipped margaritas as we watched the sun go down. After a bit Linda said:

"I like Sam."

"So do I."

"I really do think that the two of you make the perfect couple."

"I've heard it said by some that have seen us together that you and I make the perfect couple."

She laughed and then said, "I know bullshit when I hear it, but thank you for the thought."

"It isn't bullshit, Linda. I look older than I am and you look years younger than what you are and while we may be a May-December couple there doesn't appear to be all that many years between us."

"Oh come on. I'm older than your mother was."

"And I had the hots for her too."

"Oh Hermie; whatever am I going to do with you."

"Keep me around is what I'm hoping for."

She reached over and patted my leg. "Come on, baby; I need to show you how much I like what you say."

She tore me up that night and I did not want to get out of bed in the morning, but she had put me to work at her company and I did need to pull my weight. We rode to work together and on the way she told me that we would be going out that night after work.

"Where?" I asked.

"It's a surprise, sweetie. You get to spend the day trying to think of what it might be."

Work was so busy that day that I didn't have time to think about it. At work our relationship was strictly business and I rarely saw her as she went from meeting to meeting. She had lunch with a client and I didn't see her again until quitting time. As we settled into the Escalade she asked:

"Ready for your surprise?"

"I don't know. Is it a good one or a bad one?"

"You haven't any idea of what it might be?"

"Not a clue."

"Good. That means that no one spilled the beans."

She changed the subject to things going on at work and I wasn't paying any attention to where she was going. "We're here," she said and I looked up and saw that we were at Sam's house.

"Can you figure it out now?"

I looked at her blankly and she said, "You have a choice. You can be the engineer who starts the train moving or just a passenger along for the ride, but I do expect you to be the brakeman riding in the caboose."

It finally dawned on me. She was going to do a gangbang.

"Are you sure about this?"

"I am. I've wanted to do it ever since I saw the films of Sam. I think about it all the time. The kinkiest thing I've ever done was make love to you while Bob watched and I decided that I want to do something really wild before I'm too old to enjoy it. You are going to be part of it, right?"

"Your wish is my command."

"Good. I want you to be the engineer and the brakeman."

"What does that mean?"

"I want you to be the first and the last and as many times in between as you can manage."

Sam answered the door when we rang the bell and she gave Linda a big smile.

"Great. You're here. I was afraid you were going to chicken out and I'd end up having to take care of the guys."

"How many?"

"You said you wanted six including Herm so I have five here for you."

We went into the house and I was surprised to see John and Terry there behind already set up cameras. I turned to Linda and asked:

"Are you sure about this? What are your clients going to think if they see you on a porn site?"

"This isn't going up on a porn site, sweetie. Sam assures me that there will only be one copy and I'll have it. It will be something for me to look at when I'm old and grey and need to remind that once upon a time I had what it takes."

She turned to Sam. "How do we do this?"

"Just get naked and get it on."

"No," I said. "We will take it slow. I'll undress you and when you get down to stockings and heels I'll go down on you. While I'm doing that one of the others will step up and present his cock to your mouth. When I think I've gotten you ready I'll make love to you and when I'm done whoever is in your mouth will take my place and from there things should take on a life of their own."

I undressed Linda and she undressed me and then I went down on her. I knew just what buttons to push and I ate her to an orgasm while she sucked Stan's cock. After she came I mounted her missionary and was able to get her to cum once more before I came. After I pulled out and Stan took my place and Ray moved to her mouth Sam pulled me into the other room.

"She wants you to be the first one in her ass and she wants you as many times as you can get it up tonight so I'm your fluffer."

She went to her knees in front of me and took my cock in her mouth. As soon as she had me up she told me to get back in the room and tap Linda's ass so the three holing could start.

"That's what turned her on the most when she watched me. She wants to be airtight so get in there and do your duty, sailor."

"Aye aye, ma'am."

When I walked back into the room Stan had finished and Roy had moved from Linda's mouth to her pussy and Mike had taken over Linda's mouth. I had the guys pull out of her and I had Roy lie down on his back and Linda climb on his cock and lean forward to take Mike back in her mouth. I went to the dresser and got the tube of KY and went back to Linda. I worked on her butthole with thumb and fingers covered with KY and when I felt I had her ready I eased my cock into her ass. Mike and I worked up a rhythm and I fucked Linda until I came. I pulled out of her ass and let George take my place.

I went to the bathroom and washed my cock and then went into the living room and my 'fluffer' got me up again. I got Linda two more times before backing up just to watch. Sam wanted to get me up again, but I told her no.

"Linda wants me to be last so I have to save up enough to be able to do it."

Then came the biggest surprise of the night. John put down his camera and joined in. I'd never seen him take part before. He actually went three times on Linda. The first time he went into her ass and the second he had her pussy. I was watching him plow Linda's pussy when Sam came up to me.

"I don't believe it," she said. "In the three years I've worked with John he has never taken part before."

John's third time was the shocker. The guys began to fade and they started to dress and leave. Soon there was only Sam, Linda, John and me. Linda called Sam and me over to the bed and said:

"I need a big favor from you guys."

"Sure," Sam said. "What do you need?"

"Can Herm stay here with you tonight?"

"No problem; right, Hermie?"

Before I could answer Linda said, "Please, Herm? I know I said I wanted you to be first and last, but now I want John to be the last and he wants to take me home. Please?"

I shrugged and said, "You know I'll do whatever you want." I bent and kissed her and said, "Take care and have fun. Call me when I can come home."

As Sam led me to her bedroom she said, "I hope you have enough left for me. I got real horny watching Linda live out her fantasy."

"I can give you once, but that's about all. I saved myself to be Linda's last, but that's all I have in the tank."

"Betcha I can get a little more out of you."

"I sincerely doubt it."

Naturally she just had to prove me wrong, but it took her almost thirty minutes to do it.

When I was lying exhausted next to her I said, "Care to speculate on what happened tonight?"

"I haven't a clue. Like I said, in the three years we have worked together he has never taken part in anything that we did."

We fell asleep shortly after that.

***

At noon the next day Linda called and told me that I could come home.

"John drove me so my car is still there."

I told Sam I was going to leave and she said, "Linda told you that she would explain when you got home. You make damned sure that you call me and clue me in. I'm dying of curiosity."

"I need to know something. Does John know who she is? I mean does John know of my relationship with Linda?"

"As far as I know all he knows is that she is a very good friend of mine that I helped live out a fantasy. He knows she came with you and from hearing what she told you he knows that you expected to go home with her. Why do you ask?"

"Because Linda is extremely wealthy and she has men coming after her for her money and not her."

"I doubt that John knows that. He has never seen her before last night at least as far as I know. What are you going to do?"

"It isn't what I'm going to do; it is what Linda is going to do. Don't forget that all I am to her is her kept boy toy."

"You are more to her than that, Herm, and you know it."

"Another one of those "Trust me; a woman knows these things?"

"Precisely. Call me," she said as she stood on her tip-toes and kissed me.

***

When I got home I found Linda sitting at the kitchen table drinking coffee and working the New York Times crossword puzzle. I poured myself a cup and joined her at the table. She put down her pen and said:

"I guess I owe you an explanation."

"No you don't. We both know what our relationship is."

"Oh? And just what is our relationship?"

"I'm your every other weekend boy toy. We are friends with some damned good benefits."

"Is that what you really think?"

I shrugged and she said, "You are much more than that to me, Herm. You know I used you exclusively until you dropped out of sight. I've used an escort service every weekend I've come to town and I've had dozens of escorts. Some of them more than a couple of times, but you are the only one I've ever offered to set up in an apartment. If you were fifteen or twenty years older I would have tried to get you to marry me. To be absolutely honest there have been times when I've thought seriously about putting the age thing aside and asking you to marry me anyway.

"Don't misunderstand me here, Herm; it has nothing to do with love. I'm very fond of you and we fit together well and at my age that would be enough. At my age I never expected to find love again at least not like the love I had with Bob, but things changed last night."

I didn't say anything. I just sat there and listened.

"Last night something happened that I've read and heard about, but never believed. Last night while you were buried in my ass I happened to look over at John. Our eyes met and I swear to God that an electric spark jumped between us. He felt it too. When he came over to make love to me I felt it again. Something clicked between us, Herm. When he brought me home he made love to me two more times and it felt right, Herm. That's the only way I can describe it. It just felt right."

"So I guess I need to find another place to live."

"Oh no you don't, baby. I need you to be here for me if things don't work out with John. No changes other than I'll probably be dating John when I'm in town. Plus I need you to baby sit the house until the market improves. If necessary I'll take a hotel room for when I'm dating John or ask you to stay with Sam. I have a strong feeling that she would like that. In fact I'd be willing to bet that she would love to have you move in with her permanently. If you do decide to do it please give me enough notice so I can make arrangements to have the house taken care of.'

"I'm here and I'm yours until you tell me to hit the road."

"I don't know that I could ever do that, baby."

"Sure you can. What's more is that you will have to if the connection you feel to John stays with you."

"I don't know about that, lover. After all, he did meet me at a gangbang."

"Speaking of which, was it all you thought it would be?"

"And more. I'll be doing more of them. Maybe one a year when I feel the need to give myself a special treat."

"And if your new man doesn't approve?"

"I'll cross that bridge when I come to it. But again I will point out that we did meet at a gangbang. I do want to show you how much I appreciate your giving up your place last night, but my little party and the rest of my evening with John has tired me out so you will have to wait for tonight for your reward. You want to go out for dinner or stay in?"

***

The next two weeks slid by filled mostly with work and some evenings with Sam. She would usually call and invite me over for dinner saying that she made too much and hated to eat alone. Dessert was always served in the bedroom and most nights I never made it home.

Sam's days were filled with mailing out resumes and going for interviews. She had successfully defended her dissertation and was now entitled to add the word Doctor in front of her name and in fact I started calling her "Doc" and Doctor Sam even though she kept telling me not to.

Wednesday night I got a call from Linda telling me that John would be picking her up at the airport on Thursday and that she would be spending her weekend with him. She said that it would probably be at his place, but would I mind staying with Sam just in case? I told her I'd find some place to stay and then I told her to have fun and enjoy herself. I called Sam and she told me that I should know by now that I was welcome at her place any time and then she said:

"You can move in if you want."

I spent from Thursday to Sunday evening at Sam's and around six on Sunday I got a call from Linda telling me that I could come home.

That set the pattern for the rest of the summer. I basically house sat from Monday until Thursday and then stayed with Sam from Thursday until Sunday evening while Linda and John did their thing.

At one point I told Sam that I didn't think it fair that I tied her up on weekends.

"You should get out and date."

"I don't need to date. I've already found my guy. I'm just waiting for him to get his head out of his ass."

"Do I know him?"

She threw a dish towel at me and told me that I could be such an ass at times. Actually I didn't have my head up my ass. I knew what she wanted and I wasn't totally opposed, but I just didn't think I was ready to tie myself down.

***

Two things happened the week before school started back up and one of them was life changing. Linda was back in town for her weekend and I was staying with Sam. Doctor Sam had found a position she liked with a local company and since I got off work and was at her place before she got home I fixed dinner. She was all bubbly and happy when she got home and came up to me and gave me a scorcher of a kiss.

"I'm out of the porn business, baby. I sold my site and all rights to the product today. Will you call Linda and ask her to have dinner with us tomorrow?"

"Why?"

"She is in the investment business and I want some advice on what to do with the money I got from the sale."

I called Linda and she accepted the invitation saying, "John and I have something we want to share with you two so tomorrow works fine for us."

When Linda and John arrived and after I had fixed drinks for all of us Linda said:

"Since you both were in on the beginning we wanted you to be the first to know. John has asked me to marry him and I've said yes."

That prompted Sam to give both Linda and John hugs as she congratulated them. Then Sam said:

"I just wish that someone we all know would offer to make an honest woman out of me."

Three sets of eyes locked on me as I lifted my glass and said, "Here is to the two of you and may you both be forever happy," and then I took a large gulp of my drink.

The two women set off for the kitchen leaving me and John sitting in the living room.

"Why haven't you asked her?" John wanted to know.

"Asked who what?"

"Asked Sam to marry you. It has been plainly obvious to everyone from the start that from your first day on the set Sam has had eyes for only you. I'll admit that it took some time before she admitted it to herself, but that girl is yours, Herm. All you have to do is be smart enough to not let her get away."

"Oh come on, John. She is beautiful, smart, sexy and three years older than I am. All I am is a schoolboy with a year of school to finish. I don't have a thing to offer her. She can do much better than me."

"The fact, Herm, is that she doesn't want to do better than you. Again, it is plainly obvious that she has her sights set on you."

Just then Sam called us to dinner. Over dinner Sam said she had given Linda the proceeds from the sale of her porn business and that Linda was going to invest the money for her.

When Linda and John were gone Sam handed me a fresh drink and then said:

"It is time to shit or get off the pot, Herm. I've done everything but tie you down and brand you or get down on my knees and beg. Am I wasting my time? Should I push you out the door, not let you back in and get on with my life? Come on, Herm; talk to me."

"Truth time?"

"Absolutely."

"You are one hell of a woman, Sam. Sexy, beautiful, brainy – you are the total package. That's the problem. I don't think I'm good enough for you. You have a PhD for Christ's sake and I'm barely holding a B average as a Business Major. You started up and ran a successful business while still going to school and at best I'm just a flunkey where I work. I'm just a kid compared to you."

"That is absolute and utter bullshit, Herman. You have the attitude. The feel for doing the right thing. I'm violating a confidence when I tell you this, but Linda told me that you took to your job like a baby duck takes to water. She told me that you would probably be her local manager within two years of finishing school and going to work full time.

"You mention my successful business. It would probably have been even more successful if I would have had you from the beginning. You made the cuckold series, Herm. I had the initial idea, but it was your feel for what should be done and all your input that made the series as good as it turned out.

"You haven't even mentioned the important stuff, Herm. I don't know how you feel when you are with me, but when I'm with you I don't want you to go. I want you to stay with me. I look forward to our weekends together and I want more than just weekends, Herm. You know that I'm no inexperienced virgin, but I've never met any other man who makes me feel the way you do. I want to feel that way twenty-four seven, Herm. I want you, Herman. I can't say it any plainer than that."

"That's the physical and emotional side of it, Sam, but you aren't looking at the practical side. There is the age difference. You are out in the workforce now and you will be wrapped up in your job and the people you work with and yes, maybe meeting new and interesting men. I am going to be in school and doing things that students do. I'll be spending my time in classes and at the library. I'll be in study groups that I'll be bringing home with me so we can work together. I'll be working on group projects and papers with kids even younger than I am; the kinds of people you won't be able to relate to.

"Thankfully, due to the sale of the house I have enough to pay for school without having to work. The point being that I won't be able to play the part of the man of the house."

She shook her head and said, "You don't have to be the man of the house, Herman; you only have to be the man in my life. It is silly to even bring up the age gap. The gap between you and Linda is even wider than the gap that you say exists between us, but that didn't stop you from setting up house with her."

"That was different."

"Bull! The only difference is that I would be twenty-four seven instead of every other weekend."

"You are serious? You really feel that strongly about it?"

"I do, Herm; I really, really do."

"I can't believe that you want to saddle yourself with me, but I'd be a fool not to go along with it."

"You mean it? No bullshit; you really mean it?"

"I do."

She grabbed me and hugged me and it occurred to me that the word "Love" had never been mentioned. I really liked Sam, but I didn't know that I loved her and she had never said that she loved me, but what did I know about love? I remembered that once as a kid mom had put peas on my plate at dinner time and I kept pushing them to the side as I ate. When I asked to be excused from the table my mom had said:

"You aren't finished yet. You haven't eaten your peas."

"I hate peas."

"Eat your peas, Herman. You can learn to love anything. You just have to work at it."

Could it be that simple? Just work at it? Maybe I did love Sam, but just didn't know because I had no idea of what love really was. I loved my mother; I knew that for sure and I had pretty much the same feeling of affection for Sam that I'd had for my mom. Was that love?

In my mind I put Sam up against all the other girls and women I had been interested in and had been with and Sam came out on top every time. Love? I didn't know. I had some pretty strong feelings for Linda, but even there if it had come to making a choice between Linda and Sam there was a better than even chance I would have gone with Sam.

I guess it all came back to what Sam saw in me. I sure didn't think that I was anything special, but I wasn't going to argue with her. We would just have to go with the flow and see what happened. There were some things that were going to have to be addressed and so I brought them up.

"Linda was counting on me to babysit the house and I'm going to have to let her know that I will no longer be able to. Then there is the money I got from the sale of the house. I need to put a good chunk of it into another place or I'll have to end up paying capital gains on the money."

"That's easy to take care of. I want to get rid of this place. I only bought it because it had five bedrooms and a full basement and I needed all the room for making my films. I'll sell it, put my money with yours and we can buy a house that we both like. I'd like to get a house on a really large lot and with a swimming pool. How about you?"

"It would have to have room I could use as a home office or den and a full basement that I could use part of as an exercise room. And I suppose I'd like a two or three car garage."

"Why? You don't even have a car."

"Not yet, but when I turn the Escalade back over to Linda I plan on buying a Mustang convertible."

"Okay then, we have all of that covered and all that's left is a trip to the mall."

"Why a trip to the mall?"

"Because there are three jewelry stores there and you need to buy me a ring."

"A ring?"

She paused and looked at me for a couple of seconds before saying, "You do understand that we have been talking about marriage here, right?"

Actually I hadn't. I was thinking live together not marriage, but in for a penny in for a pound so I said:

"Oh yeah. Sure. It is all happening so fast that my mind hasn't caught up with things. Trip to the mall tomorrow. Got it."

"Help me do the dishes and clean up and then we can head for bed and practice what we will be doing on our wedding night."

Of course it was what we did every night I stayed with Sam, but I was going to complain?

There was a bit of a rough spot though. We had just finished our second go round of the night and I was lying beside her leaning on an elbow and looking down at her. She looked up at me and asked me what I was thinking. Insensitive of me to pick that moment and I knew it as soon as I opened my mouth, but you can't pull the words back once they have been spoken.

"I was thinking about you. I've watched you in action and I've seen how you respond and I'm wondering if I'm going to be enough for you."

"What the hell does that mean?"

"I've watched you do more than one man at a time and even though you say you feel like all you are is a piece of meat to the men, it was obvious to me that you were into it. So I wonder if just me is going to be enough for you."

"I ought to slap your face for that. I had sex with several men at one time and sex is enjoyable. Did I like it? Damned straight I did. Do I crave it? No I don't. It was just business to me. Enjoyable business, but just business. I put that business behind me when I got my degree. The only multiples that I'm interested in now are babies. At least two and you will damned well be their daddy. The answer to your question is yes; you are going to be enough for me. More than enough."

She reached for my cock and started fondling it. "I like this guy. I like him so much that I'll never do anything that might make him not want to be my very good friend."

***

After pancakes at the Village Inn on Demming Place we hit the mall and Sam found just the ring she wanted at Zales. It didn't need to be sized so in front of everyone in the store I took a knee in front of Sam and asked:

"Samantha Marie Croakly, will you do me the honor of becoming my wife?"

She said "I will" and I slipped the ring on her finger as the rest of the people in the shop clapped and cheered. I stood up and Sam took me in her arms and gave me one hell of a kiss.

We went back to her place and made slow leisurely love. Linda called at six and told me that I could come home and Sam told me that she wanted to go with me and when I asked her why she told me.

***

Linda was surprised when I showed up with Sam, not that Sam would be in the way of anything since Linda and I hadn't had sex since she took up with John. I guess the surprise was mostly because Sam had never come with me before. Sam kissed Linda on the cheek and then said:

"I'm here to share some good news and deliver what might not be good news. The good news is that I have a new decoration on my body," and she flashed her ring at Linda. Linda looked at it and then over at me and Sam said:

"Yes; he finally got his head out of his ass."

That got Sam a hug and me a kiss on the cheek and then Sam said, "Maybe we should sit down for the not so good news."

We moved to the kitchen and sat down and then Sam said, "I've thought long and hard over this and I had just about decided to mind my own business and then Herm told me about a conversation he had with you. The one where you told him why you preferred young studs instead of pussy hounds that might just be after you for your money. He didn't tell me this until after you and John were over dinner and gave us your news.

"I've known John for a little over four years. How we hooked up is immaterial, but we have worked together on my porn business almost the entire time I have known him. John has money. Not serious money like you," she said to Linda, "But he has a lot. What he told me was that when his parents died he ended up with over five million in life insurance and money from a wrongful death suit against the company whose drug impaired driver had killed his parents. He didn't go out on a spending spree, but invested a good part of it.

"Two days after your gangbang I was in John's home office and I was working with him on the sale of the porn business. John was my partner and owned twenty-five percent of the business. I noticed a magazine on his desk. It was a two year old copy of Investment Digest and it had your picture on the cover. It could well be that John knew who you were when he joined in on the gangbang."

Linda's face was showing the shock she was feeling over the news.

"Oh my God," she said, "I can't believe it. What am I going to do?"

I stuck my oar in the water at that point.

"What you do is be careful. You said that you felt a spark when your eyes met. You said that he said he felt it also. Maybe he did. Obviously on your side it has developed into something you feel great about and it could be that he feels the same way. He might have dug the magazine out after he saw you because he thought you looked familiar and finally remembered the magazine. We don't know how it went down. What the bottom line here is that we thought that you needed to know. Easy way to check out if John's 'spark' is real is to tell him who you are and that you will need a prenuptial agreement before you get married. If he balks at that, you will have your answer. The spark you felt and what it grew into may be enough that you don't give a damn about his motives and you want him regardless. Sam just felt that you needed to know and remembering the conversation that you and I had, I felt that she was right."

"It is a lot for me to think about, but you are right. It is something that I needed to know."

"There is one other thing. You are going to lose your house sitter. Now that I've gotten – as Sam so succinctly put it – my head out of my ass, I'll be moving in with her until she can sell her house and then we will go looking for a place."

"Not a problem. I'm sure that I can rent it out. When are you guys going to tie the knot?"

Before I could say anything Sam spoke up and said, "As soon as we can get the license and blood tests out of the way and find a Justice of the Peace."

"No big wedding?"

"To me a big wedding is a colossal waste of money that could be put to better use buying new furniture and appliances for the new house."

Linda looked at me and I shrugged and said, "I'm with her on that."

Then Sam said, "I will take him home to meet my family, but it will be more of a rub their faces in it kind of thing. They always told me that I would never amount to anything and that no good man would ever have me. It will do me a world of good to wave my PhD in their faces. That will be extremely rewarding since none of the rest of them made it any further than high school and my mom didn't even finish that. And then there is my being able to show off my stud and a half to them."

Linda laughed and said, "Only a stud and a half? He must not be giving you all he gave me. I'm going to miss him."

Sam snorted and said, "Bullshit! You pushed him out of your bed to make room for John. Not that I'm complaining mind you since pushing him out of yours just pushed him into mine."

"Come on, girls; lighten up. You are embarrassing me."

"Horseshit," they both said in unison and then Linda said, "Your ego is sucking it in and you are loving it."

Sam looked at her watch and said, "We need to be going, baby. I need a good night's sleep before I go to work and you and I have some business to take care of before I can go to sleep."

We stood up, gave Linda a hug and I told her I would start moving my stuff out during the week. She kissed me, gave me another hug and then whispered in my ear:

"I meant it, lover; I will miss you."

***

EPILOGUE

Sam and I were married in front of a Justice of the Peace with Linda and John present as witnesses. Sam sold her place and we pooled the money from our house sales with some money from my safe deposit boxes and paid cash for a five bedroom place on five acres. It has a detached four car garage, swimming pool, hot tub and a tennis court.

I bought a Mustang convertible and Sam who had loved Linda's Escalade bought one for herself. We turned one of the bedrooms into a home office for Sam and one into a home office/den for me and we are busy decorating a third for Jessica Marie who will be joining us in another three months.

I finished school and went to work for Linda's company fulltime and just a little after two years I was promoted to manager.

Linda never did confront John. She didn't have to. One day he told her that he knew who she was and that he wanted to turn all of his money over to her to invest and HE insisted on a prenuptial agreement to protect her. Sam was Linda's matron of honor and I was John's best man.

In John Linda had found another Bob in that John loved to watch Linda with other men the same as Bob had. Linda had meant what she said following her first gangbang – that she did intend to do more of them – and just recently she asked me if I wanted to take part in one for old time's sake and I have to admit that I was giving it some thought when Sam said:

"No fucking way!!! That part of our life is behind us and behind us is where it is going to stay! Do you understand me?!"

All I could do was shrug and say, "Yes, dear."

~~The End~~

Here is a sample from another story you may enjoy:

Family Affair

Just Plain Bob

Erotic Romance

Beth woke me in the morning with a blow job and then when she had me where she wanted me she mounted me and rode me cowgirl. When it was over I started to take a shower and Beth surprised me by joining me which led to me taking her from behind as she leaned forward against the wall.

Then, as was our usual habit, we took Laura and went to the IHOP for breakfast. The rest of the day I stayed busy in the yard, garden and garage until Beth called me in for dinner.

When I got to our bedroom I found a naked Beth reading and when she saw me she put the book down, got on her hands and knees and then looked back over her shoulder to me and said:

"Woof woof."

It was as blatant an invitation as I had ever seen so I moved in behind her and gave her what she wanted. I fucked her hard until we both got off and then I plopped down beside her on the bed. She snuggled into me, mumbled "I love you" and drifted off to sleep. I laid there staring up at the ceiling and wondered how she could say that to me while fucking my brother.

She meant it. I could tell that she meant it, but it just didn't make sense to me.

Sunday I found enough to do around the house to keep me away from Beth. I got through dinner okay and then watched some TV with Laura. I made sure that I was in bed pretending to be asleep when Beth got there.

Probably a dumb move on my part since I had no idea when I would ever get pussy again after I busted Beth. It was a weird thought on my part, but I just didn't think it would be right to play the part of loving husband less than twelve or so hours before I caught my wife with another man's cock in her and I fully expected that to happen sometime in the morning.

***

The morning was normal in that I got a goodbye kiss and a "Miss me?" when I left the house. Then it became anything but normal. I hit Wal-Mart and got a large thermos and then Stopped at the B&B Café to have it filled with coffee. I bought the local paper and a copy of USA Today and then drove back to the neighborhood.

There were four vehicles similar to mine in the neighborhood so mine parked at the end of the street wouldn't cause anyone visiting my house to give it a second thought if they saw it. I settled in with my coffee and the newspapers and waited to see what would happen. If Billy didn't show up that day I'd still be there watching on Tuesday and Wednesday and if nothing happened on those days I would make new plans.

It was getting close to one in the afternoon and I was starting to think about giving up on the day's stakeout when Billy's GMC pickup pulled into the driveway. He got out of the truck and went into the house without ringing the bell or knocking which told me that that he knew he was expected.

I gave it twenty minutes and then I drove up and parked in front of the house. I quietly let myself in the front door and just as quietly closed it behind me. I took a quick peek around the entryway wall to see if Beth and Billy were in the living room and they weren't. I moved quietly through the downstairs without finding them and a glance out onto the patio showed they were not there either. That left the upstairs and all that was up there were bedrooms and a bathroom.

I moved quietly up the stairs and not doubting for a second what I was going to find I turned my cell phone camera on. The first bedroom at the top of the stairs was Laura's and her door was closed. The bedroom at the end of the hall was the spare bedroom and the door was open and even from the stairs I could tell that it was empty.

That left the master bedroom and its door was closed.

I cautiously turned the doorknob and eased it open and found what I had expected to find. Beth was on the bed in the doggie position and Billy was fucking her from behind. They were facing away from the door and didn't see me as I took four pictures of them. When I hollered "Hey!!" they both turned to look and I got two more shots before dropping the phone in my pocket and going after Billy.

My brother was four inches taller than I was and maybe fifty pounds heavier and he had pretty much bullied me when we were younger until I got tired of it and laid him out with a baseball bat to the head when I was thirteen. He left me alone after that, but it was pretty much understood that he could kick my ass if it got to the fair fight stage.

If you enjoyed this sample then look for **Family Affair.**

Also by this Author:

The Prodigal Family: The Abbotts

Watching My Shared Wife

The Waitress and the Runaway Husband

Baiting Mr. Little

Too Hot for Henry

Chuck's Fantasy

The Redhead's Desires

Rescued at Riley's

His Every Fantasy

Open Mike Night

Pursuit for Revenge

Why Does He Do That?

Halloween & Drugs

Tracey

When Rob Met Kari

Becoming a Shared Wife, Vol. 1 –

(Wife Sharing and Other Adventures)

Becoming a Shared Wife, Vol. 2 –

(Hazardous Wives)

Becoming a Shared Wife, Vol. 3 –

(Wives Who Stray)

Her Illicit Adventures

What I Want To Do To Her

Too Fun To Give Up

Creamed

Stepping Out

Hottest Wife

Naughty Wives

Deepest and Darkest

More Than She Can Take

Jennifer's Toes

The More The Sexier

Spice Up

Cyndi

Naughty And Nice

House Of Lovers

Hungry For More

Sweet Revenge

Turning Mommies Wild: The Carriage Tales

Bought And Used

Get Me Off

The Gambler

Gail's Price

Family Affair

From the Author

WANT FREE COPIES OF MY BOOKS?
Just visit my blog and download free copies of my books:
<u>awesomeauthors.org/justplainbob</u>

Yes, I write about sluts and whores because as everyone knows, you tend to write about the things you know. And I do like sluts and whores, just not the ones that lie to me and cheat on me.

So be forewarned - if you click on a Just Plain Bob story you will be getting sluts, whores and husbands who do not kill, maim and destroy. There are other things you will rarely find in a Just Plain Bob story.

If you enjoyed any of my books then please share the love and promote my books in Amazon. I would really appreciate your honest reviews, too!

Good news is always welcome.

One Last Thing, For Kindle Readers...

When you turn the page, Kindle will give you the opportunity to rate this book and share your thoughts on Facebook and Twitter. If you enjoyed my writings, would you please take a few seconds to let your friends know about it? Because... when they enjoy they will be grateful to you and so will I.

Thank you!

Just Plain Bob
justplainbob@awesomeauthors.org

You may also like the books by these authors:

Ben E. Dorm

Mrs.
MOON
ROMANCE EROTICA

Conversation ceased when Mrs Moon entered. She paused and looked around, letting them see her as she gave the place the once over. It hadn't altered at all to her notice: ill-fitting, threadbare carpet, once blue but faded and dirtied by years of traffic, mostly scuffed and dirty work boots, all raggedy at the periphery and curled in one corner. The same old calendar hung on the wall, a bosomy young blonde smiling out, the young woman at least two years older than the year displayed in the calendar's header. A knackered settee sat against the back wall, while a remnant from some ancient kitchen stood in one corner, a freestanding unit brought in by someone to act as a surface upon which rested a kettle, a five litre bottle of water, and the makings for tea and coffee. There was a fridge next to the kitchen unit, unloved and unclean, its job being to keep milk cold during the working week as well as lager for the Friday afternoon drink-up. A low coffee table was in front of the sofa, much be-ringed by coffee and tea stains, an overflowing ashtray in its geographical centre despite the no-smoking sign on display.

"Hello, Mrs Moon," one of the men said, a stocky, grey-haired man, his hair cut very short to his scalp. The man pushed himself upright from where he'd been leaning against the fridge, his arms folding across his chest as he moved. Mrs Moon knew him to be in his late forties, the foreman of the workshop.

"Tim," she replied, acknowledging the greeting. She surveyed the assembled group, eying each in turn. "Hello, boys," she breathed.

Three of the four remaining men mumbled their hellos, the trio wearing the same garb as Tim, grease-stained, baggy overalls. They were ubiquitous twenty-something's, one of whom Mrs Moon found rather attractive. The other two were nondescript, longish dark hair in need of a trim. In Mrs Moon's eyes they were unremarkable in every way, except to serve as extra meat in Mrs Moon's diet. She couldn't even recall their names – Alan and Pete or some such. Anyway, she had no interest at all in their personal lives or their circumstances. The young mechanics were always changing, with one leaving to be replaced by another, Tim being a constant in all the months Mrs Moon had enjoyed her Thursday afternoon sojourn in their company. She nodded at the trio, two of whom were sitting in the questionable embrace of the sofa, knees high because of insubstantial support in the sway-backed piece of furniture, the good-looking one sitting on the seat of an old ladder-backed chair, his arms dangling over the back support, the chair reversed beneath him.

The fifth man, the one standing with his back to the rear wall, the man in the suit, she ignored completely.

"Are you ready?" Mrs Moon asked, moving into the room with an exaggerated swing of her hips. "I hope so," she added, facing square on to the sofa, fists on her hips. "Because I'm so fucking horny…"

If you enjoyed this sample then look for **Mrs. Moon.**

HIS WIFE *and* HER HUSBAND
SPOUSES WHO STRAY

HOT ROMANCE EROTICA
JACK RYDER

Shelly and I were always sort of mismatched now that I look back at the eight years we were husband and wife. I was always a night owl. Preferring the late night hours to write my stories when there were no distractions and the rest of the neighborhood was asleep.

Shelly was one of those early to rise and early to bed sorts. She spent her morning working out to keep her highly tuned body at its peak performance. She spent the rest of her day with her clients. Shelly was a very popular personal trainer in our little part of the world.

Things went fairly well the first three or four years of our relationship. We could laugh off our differences as amusing quirks that added to the uniqueness of our love. But after a while, those differences began to grate on us. It began to erode the foundation of that uniqueness.

Shelly was always so busy that she often left things a mess. It wasn't just a little mess either. She would leave any room she'd been in looking like a tornado had roared through. After years of cleaning up after her, I began to resent it. I felt like I was her personal maid or something.

It seemed that Shelly's biggest resentment was that I would try to get sexual with her when she was ready for bed. But she grew more and more resistant as the years went by. Often telling me she was too tired or that it pissed her off that I would get back up afterward to go do some more writing.

After a while, we fell into a routine of sorts. I stopped complaining about her messiness but became very quiet and uncommunicative when she was home. She responded by coming home later and later and curtailing our sex life to a holiday treat or as a favor when she wanted something special. Those episodes usually occurred each time I received a large bonus when one of my books did very well.

I'm sort of telling you all this boring stuff so you can get an idea of how we sort of drifted our own directions. I became accustomed to doing pretty much whatever I wanted to go do. And Shelly pretty much came and went as she pleased as well.

But you need to understand that I never once considered having an affair or seeking out companionship in any manner. I truly believed that we were just suffering through growing pains and that eventually things would straighten out for us.

I also have to tell you that I have a very active sexual drive. As time passed, I found ways to…take care of my own needs so to speak. I found ways to satisfy myself. I found there were many ways that one could have anonymous sex and there were many others that were seeking the same release.

It started out with a few harmless trips to the Adult Arcade out on the edge of town. The sign had just caught my eye one afternoon after having an argument with Shelly. She had taunted me afterward saying that the next time she would fuck me is when pigs fly.

I felt a little apprehensive when I first stepped into the arcade. Afraid I might see someone that I know and they would think I was some sort of pervert. I was surprised to see that there were nearly a dozen people milling around in the large center area that was filled with rows of videos, sex toys and sexy lingerie.

I noticed a couple of men over in the back corner by the gay magazine row. They seemed to be sizing me up as they gawked at the magazines they were holding. It even appeared that two of them were sort of petting each other below the level of the shelves.

There were a couple of middle age women that seemed like they were a little embarrassed to be here. But they were whispering requests at the counter clerk.

I figured they were here to purchase some stuff to spice up their sex life at home. I felt a little jealous as I thought of that. At least these women were trying to find ways to keep their sex life alive.

I also noticed one woman in the other back corner alone. She was holding up sexy panties as if inspecting them. But she kept looking over as if to see if I was paying attention to her. She was wearing a very short mini skirt and extremely tight pull over top. The way her nipples were poking against the tight cotton fabric, it was easy to tell she was not wearing a bra. She sort of looked like a hooker.

I noticed the hall way to the arcade with the private booths. I smiled at the woman one last time then made my way down the hall. I went to the very last booth at the far end of the hall and closed the door behind me. I quickly shoved $5 in the pay slot and selected a porn video to watch.

I just got my pants down and was gently tugging on my prick when I heard the door to the booth next to mine open and close. Moments later, I heard the sound of the machine taking money in the next booth. Then I heard a loud moaning as the porn came on in the next booth. In a few seconds, the sound became the same as the video that I was watching.

I was just getting a good rhythm to my jerking when I suddenly heard "Pssssst," coming from the wall next to me. When I glanced down, I saw a four inch hole in the wall at just the same level as my cock…

If you enjoyed this sample then look for **His Wife And Her Husband**.

AMY REDEK
HOT EROTICA

No
White
Snow

My name, though of no consequence, is Julie Winters and the younger sister of April, though her surname has now been Summers after marrying Jack, who is now my brother-in-law. How and why she married a man with that surname considering what hers had been, I never had the gall to ask her.

They had been married for almost two years. During the first year, my mother died; and after another year, my father followed her. I was then seventeen years old and since there was no will written by my father, the house and any monies in the bank etc., were then passed onto both my sister and myself.

Rather than living on my own, my sister suggested that I live in her house while we sell our parents' house. This way, we could have a bit of money each. Since I still have a year of college education and being virtually broke, I agreed to her suggestion, and so I moved in, though for that first year, I spent most of my time at my college and it wasn't until I got my diploma, did I really move in to live with my sister and brother-in-law.

I didn't know then of the desire that Jack had for me, but later found out after living with them for three months. April had gone up north to see how an aging aunt was coping, I was left alone with Jack, who told me to stop calling him brother and use his name.

That first night we were alone, he suggested that instead of me cooking dinner, we go out for that evening meal. He was the perfect gentleman then and after a lovely meal, we returned home and he suggested that we have a couple of drinks before bedtime. I'd already had half a bottle of wine and thought that a couple more drinks would be okay, so I said that it would be a nice way to round off the evening.

Now I can't say if he spiked my drinks or not, but a lot of what happened, I cannot really remember. I know I laughed a lot as we had our drinks and must have been given some kind of drug for when he pulled me into his arms as we sat on the sofa, I had no objection to him kissing me. I must have liked it, with him really being the first man to kiss me and didn't even have any qualms about having his hand fondling my breasts as we kissed.

Nor did I object when his hand went inside my blouse and had it push up my bra to release my breasts and have his hand massage them. Nor did I stop him from taking off my blouse and bra for him to kiss and nibble on my nipples. I think I enjoyed it since I stroked his hair as he sucked on my nipples and didn't stop his hand from wandering down over my stomach and moved down under the waist of my skirt to have his fingers enter my pussy.

I appeared to have enjoyed his fingers playing with me for I gave out a little cry when he pulled his hand out and didn't see him pull down the zipper of his trousers because he was still kissing me. He then took hold of my hand and guided it into his trouser that was now open. He pushed my hand inside till I felt his erection and hand him curl my fingers round that hard muscle of flesh and gently moved my hand up and down on it.

There is a gap in what I remember for the next thing I know, we were lying on the rug and I was no longer wearing my skirt but completely naked as he was. He was down in between my legs and had his tongue moving about in my pussy, licking and sucking on me. His tongue was also exciting my clit. I gave out a cry when he stopped doing that to me as it was really exciting me. He then started kissing my stomach first before slowly moving up, kissing me all the way until he was kissing and sucking on my breasts.

If you enjoyed this sample then look for <u>No White Snow</u>.

Saving Heather

HOT ROMANCE EROTICA

LILITH JONES

She went into his arms. Her kiss had been intended to be a light acceptance of his niceness. He kept it up, though, and she certainly had no reason to end it. He sucked her lower lip, and then he licked her lips. She opened them to him, but he kept licking them. She finally sought his tongue with hers. When they met, sparks flew. He pulled her to him, and she felt his firmness against her stomach.

"Oh, my love," he said when they broke. His hands went to the buttons on her blouse. She was his, and she let him strip her. He did it slowly, kissing every newly revealed inch of skin. She felt aroused, more aroused than she had been in years. She also felt cherished, cherished as not even the Rick of years ago had cherished her.

When he was kneeling and he had her jeans down around her ankles, he eased back to let her step out of them. Then he kissed her legs upward to her panties. He kissed her mound through those panties, and she felt ready for him. He eased her down on the bed.

If he'd been patience personified in removing her clothes, he was nearly a blur in removing his. Then he faced her, fully nude and magnificently male. He looked as ready for her as she felt ready for him. She pushed the panties down, and Rick took them off her feet. She spread her legs slightly as he got into bed.

He started with a kiss, though. It was a gentle, but extremely sensual, kiss. She arched her hips off the bed as their tongues met. He cupped her, holding all her femininity. As he moved his mouth from hers to her breasts, her nipple strained upward towards his mouth. He licked it, touching only the tip with the tip of his tongue. She quivered all over, and he moved to the other breast. When he sucked that nipple, sparks shot from the tips of her toes.

He thrust one finger deep inside her. Then he drew it out, very slowly, and over her clit. It was only one finger, but it went so slowly that it felt much more -- maybe a yard long. He changed breasts again and sucked deeply. The sucking and the stroking were sending heat through her. She felt as though she was being baked, and there was a fire in her womb.

He raised his head from her breast and stared into her eyes. "Heather," he said. "Heather, my love."

Then lightning crackled within her. She moaned and writhed. It went on as he kept stroking. She collapsed, and he removed his finger. He kissed her forehead and her shoulder. As her breath eased, he kissed her nose tip, and then her breasts, and then her stomach.

He again stroked her mound. He rubbed the lips there against one another, very softly. The response, however, was fire. His hand was wonderful, and his look was loving if it was searching. He had brought her delight, and she could believe he would bring her more delight. She wanted more than that, though.

"You," she said. "Please!" He rolled away suddenly. She stifled a protest when she saw that he was reaching in his drawer. She almost told him that he didn't need the rubber. She could tell, though, that this was one more act of caring. He was taking responsibility, taking care of her. Whatever the physical shortcomings, she would celebrate it as an action of the man who would never put her at risk.

Now, he was kneeling between her legs. She spread her lips with her hand and rolled her hips to receive him fully. She felt open to him.

"Heather," he said.

"Yes, oh yes."

However open she had been, she felt him stretch her more as he went in slowly. And it was slow, agonizingly slow. When he had filled her, he kissed her briefly. She hugged him with her arms and with her legs. He was in her, but she wanted to hold all of him.

He withdrew as slowly, and he felt a need for him to return. He thrust in a little faster, and she felt herself burn. As he sped up, it was never fast enough. She thrust up to engulf him as he came down. Then the lightning crashed through her again.

He withdrew half way, rammed into her, and pulsed deep within her. For a second, he was one rigid arch within her hug. Then he collapsed onto his elbows. She, too, relaxed. Her feet rested on his calves, and her hands rested on his back, but she was no longer really hugging him.

That was closeness. They were one. She was disappointed when he moved away, although the freedom to breathe was a relief. He moved off the bed and turned off the overhead light. As he came back, she heard the rubber drop into the wastebasket.

"We really need another pillow," he said as he got into bed. He lay down beside her and pulled her into a hug. He carefully spread the sheet over both of them.

"We don't really need a wider bed, though," she said. He chuckled. "Y'know . . . Maybe you don't know. I'm on the pill."

"Well, it didn't seem a good time to ask."

"It wasn't. You took care of me."

"I always will," he said. "Somebody should. You work too hard taking care of Anne. Somebody has to take care of you."

"Well, maybe, we'll take care of each other."

"That's a good idea. I love you. Seriously, if we're going to be a family, we'll have to divide up the family tasks. Probably, you should do the dividing. But give me some of the tasks of caring for Anne. Just because I don't know how, doesn't mean I can't learn."

"You do great. I might have to give her the baths and wash her clothes, but you give her kisses and protect her."

"Washing her clothes and yours can't be all that different from washing mine, and I wash mine already. Anyway, first you get the divorce, preferably with full custody. Next we get married. Then, if I can, I adopt her. After that, we'll try to get her to call me Daddy."

"I love you." Heather thought Rick's project to get Anne to call him Daddy reflected more of the story that she'd heard at the funeral than Anne's situation. Right now, Anne had two men in her life. One beat her, and she called him Daddy. The other hugged her, and she called him Rick. Anne would know which name meant love. Well, courts took forever, and four-year-olds were resilient. By the time Rick had gone through his agenda, Anne would call him anything he wanted.

"And I love you, too," Rick said. She believed him. His hand stroked up to her breast, and she patted it and held it there. "Is this what married people do?" he asked. "I mean lie in bed and talk later?"

"Well, I'm not sure that I want my last marriage to be a model." And that was an understatement. Too many of her conversations with Bill had been at the top of their lungs. "Is this what you want our marriage to be?"

"Yeah. Especially this part." He squeezed her breast very lightly. "I like holding you."

"And," she said in satisfaction, "I like being held by you."

If you enjoyed this sample then look for <u>Saving Heather</u>.

DEXTER'S
Renaissance

LEE NORTH

Hot Romance Erotica

That May picnic was the beginning of a series of dates that Michelle and I enjoyed. Sometimes to a movie or play, often for dinner, occasionally for a ballgame. It was on one of those dates that there was a distinct shift in our relationship. Until then, we had held hands, kissed lightly, and generally behaved ourselves. I think we both could feel the pressure building. It changed after we had spent a pleasant evening at a local play.

We were in her late model Lincoln and I was driving. In the past, I would stop at the Rossmoor and she would drive on to her apartment. That night she had other ideas.

"Drive to my place, Dex. It's Friday, and we've got all weekend. You haven't been to my place yet and I'd like to spend some time with you," she said, placing her hand over mine.

It didn't take me any time at all to agree and head toward Lakeshore Drive. As we neared the building, Michelle took a small transmitter from her purse and pushed a button. The open grilled gate began to rise and I drove into the underground parking area as she directed me to her numbered space. The transmitter also unlocked the door to the elevator and stairs. After waiting a moment for an available car, a door slid open and we entered with Michelle inserting a card and pushing a button marked "R."

When we stepped out of the car, a large glass window was directly in front of us and I could see we were at the top of the building. To the left was 2102 and to the right, 2101. Michelle guided me right and opened the door, stepping in and turning on some lights.

It was a very nice and apparently large penthouse suite, one of two on the top floor of the building. As I looked around I saw the trappings of affluence; fine furniture, interesting artwork, and lush carpeting.

Michelle kicked off her shoes and I followed suit.

"Dex, I'm all sticky from the humidity today. I'm going to have a shower and change. Why don't you do the same, then we can relax and get to know each other better," she smiled.

I wasn't about to decline the offer and happily agreed. She led me to the main bathroom, handed me some towels and a washcloth and told me how to work the controls on the shower system. I needed the lesson. It was a multi-head system with pre-selected temperatures. The cabinet itself was almost as big as the bathroom in my apartment.

As I soaped and rinsed, I almost expected that Michelle would suddenly appear and join me, but that didn't happen. I stepped out of the shower, towelled myself off, and dressed in my slacks and shirt. I didn't bother with socks. They wouldn't be as fresh as I was so I stuffed them in my back pocket as I headed barefoot for the living area.

Waiting for Michelle, I wandered about the spacious penthouse. There was a dining area with a very nice buffet and china cabinet, along with a large period-style table and chairs. The kitchen was through a wide passage and it too was large, with a big island and plenty of cabinet and counter space. Most houses didn't have this much room.

I was just coming out of my inspection of the kitchen when Michelle reappeared and got my undivided attention. She was wearing a black silk pyjama suit, if that's what it's called. It was floor length, very sleek with material flowing from its wide legs and arms. She had a smile for me as she approached, then stopped and swirled in a circle to emphasize the graceful lines of her attire.

"You like?" she asked, already knowing my answer.

"Very nice ... very elegant." I almost added very sexy. As she had moved to show off the garment it was immediately apparent that she was wearing nothing beneath it. Her nipples protruded clearly in front and her buttocks were perfectly outlined in back. I could feel my erection beginning to develop.

"Would you care for coffee … or perhaps a glass of wine or brandy?" she asked in a tempting tone.

"I'd like a glass of brandy, please."

"Oh, good. I'll have one too," she said, turning to move into the kitchen.

I followed her as if she was drawing me along. Perhaps it was the magnetic appeal of her, dressed as she was in such alluring garb. She reached up in a cupboard for the brandy bottle and I stepped behind her to help her. I was directly behind her now, touching her slightly with my hips and chest. On the spur of the moment, I did something I would never have thought I would do.

With the fingertips of my right hand, I lightly, slowly, ran them up her side, feeling her ribs as I went. Then, in a moment of complete recklessness, I moved my hand and gently cupped and stroked a fulsome breast. I felt her shiver from the contact but she didn't push me away or resist my touch. In fact, I was sure I heard a soft moan.

I couldn't see her face, but she had begun to lean back into me, the brandy bottle now forgotten. Her hands were on the countertop as if bracing her against an assault. My left hand joined the right in teasing her nipples and now her groan was more audible. Emboldened, I allowed my left hand to slip down over her abdomen and softly rub the silky smooth material of her gown.

I felt her backside push slowly back into me and she could certainly now feel my erection. I moved my hips to place my hardened member between her cheeks. She welcomed that with a swaying motion that only reinforced my hardness. One of us was going to have to do something soon.

It was Michelle who took my right hand and guided it inside her top, giving me access to her breasts. She pulled at the fold of the material and I felt a little pop as a small snap released the upper half of the garment.

Still holding my hand, she slid it down to her waist where another small snap gave way and the gown parted completely.

I felt her shrug her shoulders and the lovely black item fell at her feet. She was naked before me, still facing away but leaning back more urgently against me, pressing herself into my prominent manhood. Once more, I did something I would not have thought I could attempt. I intimated with my knee that I wanted her to spread her legs and she immediately complied. She understood exactly what I was intending.

I unbuttoned my pants and they too fell at my feet, my briefs following them almost immediately. I took my cock in my hand and began to stroke her already wet centre in preparation for my entry. Again, she did everything she could to help me and within a few moments I was pushing into her. Slowly and carefully at first, but her insistence gave me courage to thrust a little more and soon I was buried well inside her.

I moved a little more forcefully and quickly as she continued to encourage me. There was absolutely no doubt in my mind that this was what she had planned all along. Her voice soon joined the action, not so much with words but with little cries of encouragement and pleasure. How long it had been since she had been with a man I did not know. I only knew she was with me now, and I was reaping the reward of her pent up need.

I leaned my head forward and captured an earlobe between my lips, then licked the back of her neck as I continued to stroke into her. In response, she threw her head back, growling a pagan, earthy moan of lust, slamming her ass back into me, the smacking sound of our joining now growing louder. This was probably going to end quite soon, but I did whatever I could to hold off as long as possible.

A few moments later her moves became more erratic and we almost fell out of rhythm as she began her orgasmic journey. I stayed with her as long as I could, but I was going to finish as well and there was nothing I could do to prevent it. I felt myself release into her once, twice, then a third time. As I did, she sagged against me and I wrapped my arms around her waist so that she didn't collapse against the granite counter or on the floor.

In all my experience, limited as it might have been, I had never had a more erotic, spontaneous coupling than this. I was in no condition to continue. Michelle was leaning back into me, breathing heavily and holding my arms tightly as they encircled her. Not a word had passed between us from the time she walked to the liquor cupboard.

I'm still not sure what got into me that night. I was either very confident of myself or very reckless. Probably the latter. Nonetheless, I picked the naked beauty up in my arms and carefully steered my way out of the kitchen toward the master bedroom. When I arrived, I saw that the bed had been turned down and I carefully laid Michelle on it crosswise with her legs dangling over the side. Her eyes were open and she was staring at me, no doubt wondering what I was doing. Still, neither of us had yet spoken.

I pulled off my shirt and now as naked as she, I got on my knees on the lushly carpeted floor, my hands gently but insistently pushing her legs apart. Again, she offered no resistance. I moved between her thighs and began to kiss the flawless, smooth skin. I was about to work my way up to the place where I had just planted my seed when I felt her hands in my hair. Was this a 'stop' or a 'go?'

I could see a bit of my semen on the lips of her vagina and I wondered what possessed me to try this. What was I trying to prove? Yet, even with that question in my head, I continued. As Michelle realized what I was planning, she must have had second thoughts. That had prompted her to place her hands on my head again, trying to decide if she should put a stop to my intentions. As I made up my mind to continue, I felt her resistance lessen.

I moved toward my target and slowly, with the flat of my tongue, I began to make love to her once again. This was going to be a very different kind of penetration. I had plenty of experience with oral sex but none just after I had planted my seed inside a woman. It was too late to stop now, and Michelle was making no sign that she wanted me to.

In fact, I was bringing her back to life with my tongue and fingers. Her hips were rising and falling erratically, responding to whatever stimuli she felt. Her grip on my head tightened and I could feel her fingers in my hair. She was holding on tight, her body dancing to whatever music my tongue created. I flicked the tip of her clitoris and got the response I expected. Her hips snapped up in reaction.

I was beginning to tire … or at least my tongue was. Michelle was nearing another orgasm and I willed myself to continue. At last she let go and I could stop and rest. I crawled up beside her, lying on my back. She rolled over me and gave me a deep, soulful kiss. Whatever I had accomplished, she approved of it. I wondered if it was something her late husband had not provided.

We lay there for a while, her head on my shoulder, our legs dangling over the edge of the bed. I kissed her forehead and ran my fingers through her soft, flowing hair. Her hand was holding my now flaccid cock, not manipulating it, just holding it lightly.

"That was wonderful," she said at last. "I didn't realize just how much I wanted you and you were perfect for me."

"We took some chances tonight," I said. "That gown didn't leave much to the imagination."

"It was either that or I would just come out naked. It was a coin toss."

"Were you worried I wouldn't get the message?"

"That thought did cross my mind. I can never be sure just what you are thinking about when it comes to women, Dex. Sometimes shy, but tonight a completely different person. You took command and I was the lucky one when you did."

"You were irresistible. I'm sure that was your plan, wasn't it? Well, it worked. I couldn't resist you, so everything that happened was a result of that."

"You'll stay tonight, won't you?"

"Yes. You might regret it in the morning, but I do want to stay. I want to wake up with you."

"We've started something, haven't we?" It was as much a statement as a question.

"I hope so. Is that what you want?" I wondered.

"Yes. As little as I know about you, as little time as I've known you, everything I've learned tells me that you are right for me."

"Well, we're going to have some time to find out so let's enjoy ourselves and see where it goes. I'm not a one-night-stand kind of guy. I'm looking for something more than that."

"You wouldn't be in this apartment tonight if I thought otherwise. But now that you're here, I'm going to keep you here as long as I can."

After a few minutes, Michelle rose and padded to the ensuite bathroom, closing the door behind her. She returned a minute or so later and crawled on top of me, rubbing my still limp cock with her lightly haired sex. I began to respond to her tantalizing little game and she noticed.

"Oh … isn't that nice. Can I have some more please, sir?"

"Of course you may. Just tell me your heart's desire, young lady, and I'll try and fulfill your wishes."

"Well, after that glorious fucking you gave me in the kitchen, I think I'd like you to make love to me. Something nice and slow and lasting."

"How would you like me to start? A little foreplay, perhaps?"

"I think I've had all the foreplay I can handle tonight, Dex. I'm still carrying some of you around in me and what I really want is to have you inside me again."

If you enjoyed this sample then look for **Dexter's Renaissance.**

WANT FREE COPIES OF MY BOOKS?
Just visit my blog and download free copies of my books:
awesomeauthors.org/justplainbob